MW00981148

My Wings
Got Lost with the
Luggage

A Little Town Seen
Through the Eyes of an Angel

Mark Griffin

**This is a work of fiction. Any resemblance
to anyone living or dead is purely coincidental.**

Disclaimer

Any religious statements in this book
are <u>not</u> connected to any formal church or religion
and come strictly from the imagination of
the author to make a good story
and are not to be taken serious or
meant to be in conflict with,
or an attempt to change anyone's beliefs.

**The concepts in this book
are not an expression of the
author's personal beliefs
which will remain private.**

Mark Griffin is the author and illustrator

of thirteen children's books entitled:

The Little Squirts Books for Children

www.kidsbooksfree.com
www.amazon.com

Children's Books by Mark Griffin

1. Little Squirts Book One... the Beginning

2. Bizby and Grandpa's Desert Adventure

3. Just in Time

4. The New Library

5. The Harvest Festival

6. Here Kitty Kitty

7. Rosy's Daydream

8. Rocky's Dayoff

9. Philo and Phoebe's Fragrant Freenkert Farm

10. All That Was Old Is New Again

11. Who Did It?

12. The Old Speelock

13. Gramples

Table of Contents

Table of Contents Continued:

Dedicated

To my dear sweet wife, Patty, who helped edit
this book without complaint
and laughed even when
I wasn't funny.

INTRODUCTION

This book is a work of fiction. The characters have been molded, embellished and drawn from the vast array of people I have bumped into over the last sixty years.

My stories were formulated from bits and pieces both real and imagined. A great percentage of these stories are based in truth and real-life experience but most of the icing on the cake just came along for the ride when I took the time to write it down. I write just like I paint. Start in the corner; work your way out and hope for a finish near the door.

What I am really trying to say is: *None of you who recognize yourselves are entitled to a royalty, so don't even think about it!* You were lucky to be noticed in the first place. You probably didn't even think I was listening as you jabbered away! So here is "a heartfelt thank you" for being the character that grabbed my attention and made me laugh.

Go ahead, call me a cheapskate. I'm not easily offended. If you are willing to take the amount of time and effort it took to write this book, then you can have one of *my* stories for free too. I am sure if we met, I must have deluged you with at least one tall yarn, so go ahead and change the way I told it to fit your style of writing and sell a million copies. Just remember; anything over a million and you will be introduced to my lawyer who will demand, at the very least, a gift-basket. I like guacamole and please no alcohol.

On a more serious note: The concept of God in this book was taken from my own imagination. It is not necessarily how I, as the author perceives God, but how the character and narrator, Griffin Marcus sees Him.

Griffin will refer to God in the male form and will also include a Goddess in the female form who, in this story, is God's Wife, a *Mother in Heaven*, so to speak known as Mrs. God. To her close friends and angels she prefers "Mrs. G. or just plain Lorain."

It would just be too complicated to try to be politically correct, so give me a break and try to remember that this story is fictitious and totally harmless.

This book is not meant to make any religious statements or conflict with anyone's idea of the hereafter or what my narrator calls the *Other Side*; it is pure imagination and meant to be fun.

If you want to fight over your viewpoint, please go bother somebody else about it. I don't have the time or patience. Please try to control yourself and find a more productive hobby. Love as much as possible and soon you'll find that hounding others over philosophical beliefs is really not that much fun anyway. Your friends will find you less annoying and you might get invited to dinner more than once. The same statement applies to all you 24-hour news junkies. When are you ever going to learn?

Chapter One
How is Procrastination Possible in a Timeless World?

My name is Griffin Marcus. I am an angel. Not the best of angels and not the worst. Sort of an upper mediocre variety with a simple job to do.

In Angel School I received mostly Bs and Cs. I got a *satisfactory* for sportsmanship and general behavior with a great big *unsatisfactory* for –"makes good use of time."

God sat me down the other day and told me I had better "get my butt in gear." Yes, this is a direct quote. Did you think your Uncle Harry had a corner on slang and profanity? I hate to be the one to break the news but here it goes… God invented our language and all of its color. He also invented the Devil to take the blame.

Narrator's Note: There will be almost no profanity in this book so don't worry. Your kids will probably hear more on the bus ride home from school than in this book. My wife can testify that I can swear as good as any truck-driver but I just prefer to tell a story without it. – Griffin Marcus

I am not only good at procrastination; I am easily side-tracked as you can see.

It seems God has a whole lot of work lined up for me, and I, being a professional procrastinator, and I do take a certain amount of pride in the title, am, as usual, getting way behind.

It's not easy to argue with God especially when you are face to face and He has just picked up the tab for a delicious dinner, told you some terrific stories that made you laugh, totally put you at ease and made you feel incredibly loved.

I can tell already that you are sitting there with that look of confusion on your face so I better explain my situation a little bit better.

God loves me, forgives me, and makes me feel warm inside, but He has made it clear that His patience is wearing thin. He likes to take angels like me on a quick tour of all the great places in the Universe like the sewers of Bangladesh where "I could be working next" if I don't get to work. He always tells me it's *my choice* and up to my *free will*. God has a way of making it sound nice no matter what.

I have been hanging around Heaven for the last hundred years or so, listening to a lot of harp music, traveling through space and wormholes, checking out the wonders of the universe; sort of an extended angel vacation. It's one of the perks. But sometimes I feel as if I just arrived yesterday. I think it has to do with that pesky little memory eraser that comes with space travel and rebirth. God told me He created the *brain-fade* "to give us all a fresh start and not have any left-over pre-conceived notions."

Sorry, I am not allowed to tell you what Heaven is really like. You'll just have to use your imagination. But believe you me, it is nothing like you ever imagined. It's way better.

On the *Other Side*, as it has sometimes been labeled, and for all intents and purposes will be labeled as such for this book (what's in a name anyway?) there is no concept of time but the present, and right now I am in a little trouble due to procrastination.

You would think that if there wasn't any sense of time it wouldn't make any difference how long it takes for me to get around to getting started, or how long it will take to finish a project.

So file that under: *"WHAT? HUH?"* I can't come up with any good explanations. It is just another one of God's paradoxes that we will probably never understand even though some people spend their lives thinking they had it right. After death, a fading memory works in reverse; right down to the periods and commas. Nothing is left unremembered and it is a bit unnerving. But like everything else, once you know what to expect, you kind of look forward to reviewing your last life. The really good times are always fun to relive. It's like going to Disneyland over and over when you finally got tall enough for the big people rides.

Most people, even the ones who we didn't like, just wake up on the Heaven side with kind of a confused look until they see someone they recognize, which is actually everybody and then they start to laugh which lasts for quite awhile and then they run off to the nearest beach and take it easy for a couple hundred years. You meet the nicest people relaxing, telling weird life-stories on a tropical coast. It's a good thing regret is not emphasized.

Do I sound a little rebellious? Sorry, conforming to the status quo is not one of the better parts of my angelic nature. Sometimes I just can't help getting a bit crabby when I start out on something new, especially if it wasn't my idea. I guess I'm a little too used to being independent, if there is such a thing.

I can't help it. Personally, I probably wouldn't have come up with a project like this on my own. Paperwork has never been one of my strong points. I thought of blaming it all on Lucifer but he and I have met on several occasions and believe you me, you don't want to get him riled. (And if you think *you*'ve got problems, you should meet his wife! I don't know which one is winning but it is a real close race.)

I am an artist and a musician, not a writer. Not to give away the ending but I am glad I finally got started on this thing and it is turning out to be a lot of fun. God always said "trust Me" but do we ever listen?

Today has been an interesting day. God just gave me a new state-of-the-art mini-computer (complete with solar batteries and a game port). Yes me, an angel that just spent a short lifetime on Earth in the 1890's. I'm still recovering from the saddle sores. I am, however, convinced that this damned so-called *high tech machine* was Lucifer's idea. I hope it comes with plenty of aspirin. I'm getting a headache just trying to figure out how to turn it on. The label on the cover says I get an eternity of free time on the Universal Information Superhighway and free technical support with no waiting. "Whoopee!" Or should I say: "Yahoo!"

You wouldn't believe what *our* Internet looks like! I have been doing my best to avoid technology by living on planets that still think a black and white photo is a miracle but still savvy enough to have invented the toilet. (I do have priorities.) I don't know if I'm ready for high tech.

God is the one who invented "upgrades," including all the mistakes in the last version. Sorry Bill Gates.

God has always said if He had given us everything up front, we would have nothing to look forward to. God keeps us in the creation loop by letting us work out our own style but God's version of Windows is way better. Not just a window; it's a whole sky. Oh well, like it or not, here goes.

After an hour spent looking for the "ON" switch I have realized my limitations.

Mark Griffin

CHAPTER TWO

Comfortable,
Like an Old Pair of Sneakers,
and Smells a Bit Like it Too

This story begins in present day Parker Town high in the Rocky Mountains…. The turn of the twenty-first century has arrived plus a couple of decades. I have made a comfortable nest in a big old stone building that was built by the military for some long lost reason in this little town that doesn't show up on too many maps. You can Google it and it won't show up either. This is a fictitious story trying very hard to be real.

The people that wind up in Parker Town are a mixed bunch of characters. They consider Parker and the surrounding mountains to be one of God's best creations and think of this tiny roadside attraction as paradise found.

The town is comfortable like an old pair of sneakers and smells a bit like it too depending on what time of the year it is. Spring thaw means a winter full of doggy dew coming into bloom. That's when we really know spring has arrived. "Awe the smell of canine intestinal fluids…It must be spring!" Lucky for us, all that is organic dries up and blows down the mountain by the end of May replaced by some of the freshest, crispest cool air on the planet.

The building I live in was built in the 1830s out of granite and logs from the surrounding mountains mixed with flagstone, tin and brick; an awesome structure that sits at the edge of our little town, literally on a cliff of solid granite overlooking the valley five thousand feet below. The elevation here is over eleven thousand feet. The air is thin and so are most of the pocketbooks.

My Wings Got Lost with the Luggage

Parker Town is not a center for industry so most people who live here think of creative ways to have money coming in from somewhere else, which may include several forms of welfare. Most of these folks are not in too big of a hurry to talk about it but if you need advice on how to get money out of the government *who spends too damn much on bombs anyway*, there are plenty of locals who know how to work the system without really working at all. The rest who actually work live off the tourist trade, as skimpy as it may be, or just buy, sell, and barter goods with the locals.

I am not alone in my love for this little section of paradise. My home is in the biggest building in town. The main room is three stories high with a wonderful observation tower. I live in the tower. The view is spectacular. I think it was originally used to keep an eye out for forest fires because there weren't any hostile Indians in this area. The town stayed pretty quiet except for the occasional hunters, outlaws or horsemen who got lost on their way to California. You really had to be lost to find Parker Town.

In the 1890s when I lived there the first time, the latest strangers in town would usually spend the evening getting drunk and creating a nuisance for the local sheriff who got a kick out of sneaking up behind them with a roughhewn nightstick. They would wake up in a heap at the edge of town with an unusually large headache, wrapped in a blanket from their saddle bags thinking they must have had too much to drink. Another drink usually cures a good head-banging hangover. The sheriff, being the big-hearted nice guy that he was didn't like trouble so he would always leave the boys with a half bottle of cheap rot-gut and a map that showed how to get off the mountain.

Many things have changed in Parker since the 1890s but once in a while the local cop has to *recreate tradition* when certain elements creep out of the hills and think the town "ain't exciting enough." Not too many of these characters claim Indian descent. Our local Indians own a casino and a ski resort about fifty miles from here and come by once in awhile in their Mercedes SUV to see what the "old west used to look like."

Lately the teenagers who live here have been sneaking up to the upper deck of my building to launch hang gliders. Their parents had a fit when they found out and raised holy hell with the latest owner.

Up until just a few months ago the building was left empty, abandoned and rotting. "Just another tax write-off for some out-of- town landlord." The new city council passed a law that said in a nutshell, if you owned any kind of structure that is left unoccupied for more than a year, the city could come in, declare eminent domain and take it over; either selling it at auction or tearing it down. The building was sold last year for the umpteenth time. Hope the new owner comes up with a plan soon.

One guy who bought the building re-sold it five times. He would take in a large down payment and when they couldn't make a go of it he would repossess. Over and over he has collected enough to completely pay off his original investment without lifting a finger or using any of his own money. He said his life was based on failure. Every time the newest owner "failed," he came out smelling like a rose. He still refuses to fix up the building because if he did, it would kill his cash-cow.

There is a kind of unspoken camaraderie in our little town in the mountains that ties the population of less than fifteen hundred people together like a loose woven sweater that keeps you warm but there are still a few holes in it. Confident in the fact that they have a little piece of the planet few others will ever experience, they argue over who is the "most local" and who has been here the longest. Most residents lie about it and the ones who really are locals don't give a damn. Local or not you still have to be tough to handle a winter in Parker Town at over eleven thousand feet.

Quite a variety of characters can be seen coming and going on Parker Town's one main street. Some for only a day, others make it their life. There is one bus a week (the old-timers claim that it only goes *out* of town) and a narrow gauge railroad that winds its way out of the valley and up the mountain on weekends full of tourists. The shops sell them stuff they'll never use, *"created by the hands of local artisans."* Some of it looks like it came from the Buck and Half Store in Denver because that is precisely where it came from. Repackaged and placed in a western motif; most people don't know the difference.

The tourists from Denver that see it for what it is just wink at the shop-owners and watch with a smile as a one-dollar item sells for five bucks "on special at fifty percent off." Most of this junk has been more than likely created by some seven-year-old in China or India, but if you "take off the tags and scratch in your signature no one will ever be the wiser."

Most of this crap gets sent to relatives to impress them with the fact that someone in their family was successful enough to have had a vacation in some exotic place. Later on when they come to visit they wonder why such a "lovely treasure bought with hard-earned money" isn't on proud display in the recipient's living room. Some of this stuff, if it doesn't end up in the trash occasionally comes back to the giver in the form of a re-gift but no one says a word as they wrap it up and send it to someone else. The shipping accumulated on the journey probably exceeds the original cost.

My job is to watch over the citizens of Parker Town and keep a loose record of the town's *going's on*. I carry the title of Head Guardian Angel. It is a great title since I am also the *only* guardian angel. I love the job (except for the damned paperwork). Most of the time, I just fill out a form or two. But now God wants me to write a book! There's a whole lot of other stuff I would rather do than write a damned book. (That's me in the background grumbling and feeling sorry for myself.) Why couldn't God just give me a voice recorder? (He probably doesn't want to hear all that blubbering either!)

I have had this job over a hundred years and I still don't have a secretary. Maybe technology will upgrade my life now that I have a computer, if I can break away from the games I found preloaded.

God and His Wife have a great sense of humor and like to see me have fun. They also like to distract me any chance they get. They are always messing with me. I just know it!

I still can't, for the life of me, figure out why I'm supposed to write down what happens here in Parker Town but I get the sneaking suspicion that there may be a movie in the works. I love movies!

Chapter Three

Just a Minor Chemical Imbalance, Nothing to Worry About

In 1893 a young man who had barely turned twenty-one came bumping into Parker Town in a beat-up old one-horse wagon filled with pipes and pieces of an ancient organ he had carefully removed from a burned out church. With determination and a lot of bailing wire he assembled Parker Town's first live entertainment, cafe, saloon and brothel. He played the pipe-organ while a couple of other musicians with varying degrees of talent fiddled, blew horns and banged the drums while his customers "raised the roof."

It was a friendly place on Saturday night and as close to "Hell on Earth" as it could get on Sunday morning when earth-shattering hangovers took the place of gaiety.

His famous flapjacks and unlimited black coffee were a welcome sight. He made more money on his hangover cures than he did on the batch of two-day-old whiskey that flooded the place the night before.

All good things must come to an end. Three years after the grand opening a crazy woman who claimed he had left her with two kids and an unpaid mortgage in Denver caught up with him in his room and shot him in his sleep.

The night watchman didn't bat an eye as he handed the pretty lady a key. She told him that she was the owner's "sister and won't he be surprised!"

I am (or was) this man. My name is Griffin Marcus. This is my story. However, I must fill in a few of the facts before you get confused. First of all, that was *not* my ex-wife or sister. She really *was* crazy and one of the first people I met on the Other Side. She's still a handful and must be kept at an arm's length even in Heaven.

I must have been well liked considering the fact that the judge hung her the next day for killing me. I thought it was a nice gesture on the part of the town's people.

Since we ran into each other on the Other Side it has been a bit nerve-wracking getting to know her. It turns out on Earth she had one of those chemical imbalances we hear so much about nowadays. Of course, nobody in the 1890s knew a thing about it. Back then they just thought she was nuts and hanged her anyway.

I know all about forgiveness. I learned it from God when I got a review of my life. Lucky for me God was willing to forgive me after all the crazy stuff I had done.

I'm just glad she shot me in my sleep. I didn't feel a thing. Although, I was a bit surprised on waking up dead. She also shot my poor old hound-dog Andy (Andrew Jackson), with the very same bullet. It went right through my head and into his. I think they hung her more for killing the dog. I can just hear it: "By George...saloon keepers are a dime a dozen, but shootin'a good dog! Now that's a crime worth hangin' for."

Andy woke up on the other side too and damned if dogs don't have the ability to talk over here. He's had a lot of pent-up stuff on his mind and has been unleashing it (sorry) on me ever since.

That'll teach me for that time I forgot and left him over at Widow Sheridan's house. She fed him non-stop for three days. Darn near killed him. But I love him. He's still my best friend. He gives me someone to share the afterlife with who is always glad to see me no matter what kind of a rotten mood I'm in. Of course, now that he can talk I wish he would get crabby at least once in a while. Used to be, all he did was run around in circles yapping and wagging his tail. Now he gives me a full-scale explanation of his day. There are some things that are a lot better left unheard (or unsniffed as the case may be!) And yes! Dogs do like the smell of a good butt. It's just as embarrassing here on the Other Side as it was on Earth but God loves all the little animals and has no intention of making any changes. I even spent a vacation on a planet where all the critters could talk. You should hear what a spider has to say just before you suck him up in the vacuum cleaner. It's not pretty.

So I woke up dead, but not in what I thought was Heaven. I asked one guy here, "When do I get to go to

Heaven?" All he said was, "Are you happy?" I said "Yes, I guess." He said, "Then you're in Heaven."

The fact is, everything on the Other Side is pretty similar to where you just came from but the surroundings only *look* solid. I can walk through walls fly wherever I want to go. It takes some getting used to when you go back to a planet like Earth and find yourself banging into just about everything until you acclimatize.

There is no shortage of people or things to do on this side so I am not lonesome or bored. Far from it. I do recall going through an incredible light tunnel but after reviewing my life and saying "howdy" to a few old friends and relatives not to mention a nice stay on the beach, I arrived back in Parker Town at the turn of the 21st Century to more or less finish up a life that was taken away too soon.

I loved the light tunnel. It was beyond cool. Somebody said God does that one more for effect than anything. It was awesome! And really took the edge off dying. Rumor has it; God is coming up with a new one for angels going to different levels. Can't wait to see what the Old Man has in mind.

Who am I to question God's motives? Besides I am having a ball. I'm out of debt. The place I built a hundred years ago has changed a lot but I still get to enjoy the old pipe organ.

Oh yeah, one of the best parts of being an angel; I have been given the privilege of being able to come back as a human observer. This means I can change bodies as I see fit and come and go as I please. I am always the newest stranger in Parker Town.

They say this is just one of the many steps to Heaven. I'm still on my way to becoming a full-fledged angel, you know, earning my wings and all that. But in the meantime I am very content. At least at this point I know God loves me and has given me the greatest gift, that is, the choice to fulfill my dream or even change my dream if I want to. I am having a lot better time than when I was an earthling.   No hangovers (or dreaded social diseases!). Fact is, over here I never even catch a cold, unless I need sympathy.   I should get an Oscar for some of my time spent in the local hospital. There is something to be said for sympathy from a pretty nurse.

Most of Parker Town turned out for my funeral (probably for the free drinks). They all chipped in and put a little plaque over the entrance to my establishment that read:

In Memory of Griffin Marcus
May He Find His Way to Heaven.

I thought it was a little pretentious, but then again my ego found it to be inspiring. I still like to go by the sign now and then just to wonder if they really meant it. Come to think of it, those people are all over on this side now. Considering the fact that most of this story happened over a hundred years ago.

I see a few of the old gang once in a while. We laugh about hard times and promise to keep in touch but you know how that goes.

Being so called *dead* does have its benefits. At least on this side there are no unlisted numbers. If you think good thoughts about someone for a few minutes they just show up. That also works in reverse so a word to the wise.

A little more background probably wouldn't hurt. First of all, I fell in love with this little town the moment I saw the sun rise over the 14,000 foot peaks. It was a few years before the turn of the 20th century and I was about to run across a string of good luck that would really change my life.

I was living in the cheapest room I could rent in the city, 21 years old, 230 pounds, six foot four and hungry almost all of the time. An old negro man taught my mother to play the piano and also taught my dad the 4-string banjo and harmonica. At an early age they taught me to play and gave me a life-long love for music. Fishing, hiking and climbing mountains were high on that list too.

I had a great booming voice and scratched out a living playing weddings, funerals, churches and saloons with my parents. We had a great harmony. It didn't matter to me where we played. If you paid, we played. My mother always finagled a meal. We would trade for dinner, drinks or "whatever ya got." Sometimes it would be a couple of live chickens or a fresh-killed deer. I liked that idea. If I wanted a raise, I'd just eat or drink more.

My Wings Got Lost with the Luggage

The pay for musicians wasn't always great, so I supplemented my income by arm-wrestling in neighboring towns with a crazy buddy who not only talked me into it but trained me in the art of the con.

We would drive to the nearest town in a beat-up wagon that my friend had won in a poker game. He would drop me off at the edge of town and head for the nearest saloon or church. Bingo was real big back then. If they didn't have a saloon, anyplace that people gathered was all right with my buddy, Michael Penbrook.

At 20 years old, Michael was five foot three and built like a tree stump. He had a shine in his eyes and a smile that would have made a used car sales manager hire him in a minute. He used to say "with my red hair I can pinch any lady on the behind and keep her smiling." I'm still not sure what red hair had to do with it but darned if it wasn't true. He could back down the meanest, nastiest, ugliest bastard in town and all he had to do was put both hands in his pockets lean back his head and kick out a belly laugh. I could hear him clear down the street. The trouble was, he used to do it in his sleep and darn-near scared me half to death the first time I heard it.

I was more than amazed by the shear nerve of this kid. Even if we raked in a fortune or came home broke, I still had more fun than I thought possible. I used to hang out with Michael just to see what he would come up with next. I swear, I think that boy rarely slept.

One of our favorite ways to *do business* was to send Michael in first to kind of "warm up the crowd." He would challenge the biggest guy in the place to an arm wrestling contest to set the mood. Naturally he'd lose.

I would make a grand entrance a few minutes later. At 6 foot 4 and a couple hundred pounds, I towered over almost everyone. Add cowboy boots with 2-inch-heels. I looked like the perfect candidate for the next contest. I'd play like I'd never done it before and go on about how thirsty I was and how if someone could at least buy me a drink, I would consider the offer.

In the meantime, Michael was going around making bets with everyone in the place on the local hero. He had made friends and wanted to stick by them. He'd have the place in a frenzy. Money flying all over the place, egos being boosted and whiskey flowing like water. He went as far as to work deals with the bartenders to keep the excitement flowing as long as possible, for a percentage of course. Michael was a master of timing.

The magic moment would come. I would beat a few of the smaller guys and then take off my shirt just for effect. The biggest lug in the joint would step up to the plate. We would look each other in the eye. I had a low growl that made the crowd go wild. Somebody would blow a whistle. The first split second creates a strange kind of silence as the two arms start to bulge. In arm wrestling terms, it's an eternity getting set for the kill. I found a way to relax and let the other guy do the work. Just breathe easy, lock your arm and wait until he wears down. It saves on a lot of torn muscles and gives a short advantage if you really are a little weaker than the opponent. My fingers were so strong from playing the piano that even if the guy's arm was stronger than mine I could make the fight last longer by squeezing the daylights out of his digits. Of course in these fights it didn't matter. I always lost because Michael was betting against me. I still had an ego and didn't want to lose by much. The local hero would come out a winner and everyone in the place would be happy. I'd claim that he "cheated" and storm out the door. Fifteen or twenty minutes later Michael would pick me up around the corner and we'd head for new pickings.

This turned out to be a pretty good way to make a buck as long as we never did the same place too often. There were a lot of little bars and taverns within a hundred miles of my home filled with egos ready to be stroked.

I had saved up a good chunk of cash and was ready for something new when Michael came over and said he was leaving for California. If I wanted to go, it would be all right with him.

I'm glad I made the decision to stay. I received a few letters but after a while they quit. I ran into him again on the Other Side. Amazing how dying can change a person. He was still a laugh a minute but apparently had gone through a few hard times before getting killed by a large bull down in Mexico. It wasn't even a bullfight. He had wandered drunk into the pen, fallen asleep and four bulls trampled him to death trying to get at the feed trough. Not much glamour there. Oh well, once you pass over to this side you find out how few deaths are staged the way we would like it anyway.

Chapter Four

Of Course He's Crabby, He's Old, He's a Genius, He's Entitled

You are probably wondering how the wagon full of pipe-organ parts came into my life.

I was climbing around the mountain trails looking for a good fishing hole when I ran into an elderly gentleman from some little European country I'd never heard of. He didn't speak much English and my formal education was not too far past the fifth grade but he impressed me with the fact that he could tie a fly like no one I'd ever seen. Success measured by a string of trout in a bucket nearby.

The old man invited me back to his home and showed me a whole bunch of weird gadgets he had invented and built. If you could think it up, he could build it; an amazing craftsman. He owned all the right tools, several of which he had designed and built himself. I was immediately fascinated by this man.

I ended up trading my labor for a room in his house. Not much was required. Life was a bit slower back then. I was a great cook and he liked to eat. So other than that I was more or less around to do the heavy lifting whenever he required it but not much else. We were both a bit rough around the edges and made a good team.

The very first day I was just settling down to a good book on the front porch when the whole house shook. I almost jumped out of my drawers. Incredible, loud music was pouring out of every nook and cranny. I ran down the basement stairs and there was old Jonathon sitting on a bench in front of four keyboards and a set of foot pedals. His wife was smiling ear to ear and had a dreamy look in her eye.

I looked around and could see the whole basement was filled with organ pipes. Unbelievable! I had never seen or heard anything like it. Besides that, he could *really* play. I knew right then and there I had to learn to play the organ. He was so proud of his creation that he agreed to give me lessons if I would help him move the whole thing to a church nearby. I have never been so excited in my life. I could play the piano pretty well, but this thing was like playing a whole orchestra.

We spent the next month un-assembling, packing and reassembling hundreds of parts and hauling them over to the church. I could hardly wait to hear this thing play again. Jonathon was ecstatic. I was over the moon! I don't know if he was working me or I was working him. We both went crazy day and night hardly stopping to eat or sleep. His wife finally brought everything to a halt and forced a hot meal down us. We were so oblivious we probably could easily have starved to death.

I was amazed at the amount of talent this little man possessed. He was barely five feet tall, built like an ox and just about as headstrong too. He was adamant when it came to details and watched me like a hawk. He knew every piece of that instrument by name.

At first his abrasive personality bothered me until I came to the realization that I was in the presence of a genius. From then on his abuse went right over my head and a healthy new respect grew without shame. He could build just about anything. He had forgotten more than the average man could say he ever knew. Jonathon could also perform over five hundred songs right from memory. He was the master. I was the grasshopper. I was feeling more honored by the day to just be in the shadow of such a man and gain the knowledge of a lifetime.

How did I end up with the organ you say?

Have patience. Actually the organ that I brought into Parker Town was a different one. Spending time with Jonathon gave me the love for the instrument and a desperate urge to learn how to play with his style and expertise. It took a few more years to actually find another one to buy. My teenage years were spent learning and mastering the art of piano tuning and repair; a great way to make a living. In those days there were pianos everywhere. Lucky for me, most of them were out of tune.

Jonathon started my lessons as promised on an old calliope that he had taken in to repair. The man that owned it had died and no relatives claimed it. It was ancient, covered with cracking gold leaf and red paint. It came from a long line of German craftsman, powered by steam and used for the circus parades. You could hear it for miles. I made a lot of enemies practicing on that thing but also made a lot of friends. Everyone wanted to try it out. The biggest problem was the volume. It had two volumes, loud and extremely loud. We finally sold it to a traveling sideshow just before the mayor had us arrested for keeping the local chickens from laying eggs, breaking windows and generally disturbing the peace.

To practice, I opted for an old air-pump pedal organ the old man had refurbished. The Mayor was happy and I was kept saved from going to jail.

I was getting pretty good. Early on, I discovered that women love to be sung to. I needed all the help I could get in the dating department so I learned a bunch of romantic songs and quickly earned a bad reputation as a womanizer. A title I am still quite proud of. Lucky for me I could run real fast and most drunken husbands are a lousy shot.

Getting back to the pipe organ....

The largest building in Parker Town was named for Major Parker who built it for the military. The original name of the town was Fort Parker but it got changed after the town outgrew the fort.

The building has survived a whole bunch of different renovations, name changes, and city councils who wanted to tear it down. One committee even went as far as to have a study made to find out what it would cost to raze the building. Turns out it was more than the whole town was worth. It would cost more to tear it down than to leave it up.

The old locals still call it the "Monstrosity" or the "MT Building" for short (pronounced *empty* because of its vacancy rate). I'll just call it the MT Building from now on to keep us from getting confused.

The first time I laid eyes on the MT Building I was in love. I don't know what it was, but there was this certain something intangible that just kicks off the hormones when you see your future open up right before your eyes.

I knew that future had arrived. The building was vacant and a sign said: *Owner Will Finance No Money Down to the Right Person.* I knew I was the *right* person if I could only convince the owner.

That day I met with Mrs. Rache, the person in charge of the property. She filled me in on the background of the building and what it needed to come up to legal and livable codes.

We took a tour of the grounds. The place was huge. Over 20,000 square feet on the ground floor. It had been a lot of things over the years but mostly it had been empty. The dust was thick and the smell of rat dung hung in the air. We came across a couple of bums living in one of the rooms, but instead of kicking them out we made them the night watchmen to keep other bums out. They couldn't believe their good fortune. They were welcome as long as they kept the fire in the fireplace and not in the middle of the floor.

The main hall was a rustic structure with ceilings three stories high. At one time this was a theatre and you could still see where the stage had been turned into storage space. All in all it was a collage of strange ideas that all seemed to have been lost in time. For some reason unknown to me, I could see the finished product clear as day in my head and it was wonderful. I knew this was my little piece of heaven. Even though it looked like hell at the time.

Mrs. Rache sat me down and smiled as she looked through the paperwork. "We've sold this building five or six times in the last 20 years. Every time the latest buyer gives up and defaults, the owner takes it back. He's made more money repossessing this property than he paid in the first place.

The present owner, Bernard Baker is 93 years old, quite wealthy and has no family. "Just between you and me, I think if you explain your idea in detail, play to his heart and be as sincere as possible; I think he would go along for the ride," she said with a smile. "He certainly doesn't need the money. Personally I'd like to see somebody do something with the place. Your idea is as good as any I've heard. To be perfectly honest, there is no one in line."

We went over to the owner's house. Mr. Baker was sitting on the front porch having a cup of something that smelled a lot like Scotch blended with a very little drop of coffee. It was only 8:30 in the morning. He was in a great mood, so we spent the next hour and a half kicking around old war stories and heroes of bygone days. I was surprised to see an old dusty grand piano in the living room. He took a couple of naps while I spent the day tuning it, shining the wood and repairing little parts. It was a beautiful old Steinway and just to touch such a work of art made me feel special.

I found a pile of dusty music sheets in the bench and proceeded to bring him to tears. After that we were best buddies. He hadn't had a friend in the years since his wife died and to be honest, I got a kick out of his stories even though by the time the day was over I had heard several un-matching versions.

By the end of the day Bernard Baker was calling me "the son that he never had." I was calling him "Dad" and by the end of the week we were both making plans for the building. Bernard loved the idea of the pipe organ and would give me a sly wink every time I mentioned the brothel. His taste for whiskey went unsaid. His heart couldn't take the extra excitement though and gave out a few weeks before opening. Lucky for me he left a will. I was the only beneficiary. The property was all mine, lock, stock and barrel.

I met Bernard Baker on the other side right after I was shot. He got a good laugh out of that. He told me he was really glad I had come along. I made the last part of his life a real joy. He had died with a smile on his face.

After the graveside service which was very quiet, I moved into his house, took over his bank account and started formulating plans for the old MT Building. Turns out he was pretty well off and at that time there was no inheritance tax. I was a borderline millionaire. He was a relative stranger to the town and had kept to himself so no one seemed to care that I had walked into a fortune.

I had a portrait of Bernard taken from an old photo and painted by a local artist placed in the foyer. People would come up and ask who he was. I made a game out of making up new stories. One day he was a war hero, the next day he was a scoundrel, all in the name of fun. I think he would have approved.

One of the first things I did was to have the MT Building cleaned from top to bottom. We stripped out the old broken furniture and had a bonfire in the square. I invited the whole town; that is, all one hundred and seventeen people including the dogs.

It was a giant barbecue that nobody will ever forget, especially Marge, the owner of the general store next door. I made a rich lady out of her. We bought all of our supplies for the business through her. She made so much money that she bought her own railroad car to haul the stuff up the mountain from Crawford. Later she had it outfitted for parties and ran into Denver with her "society gals." They would get drunk and talk dirty about men all night on the train. The next morning they would get all dressed up and hit the stores, acting as sophisticated as they knew how. This went on for quite awhile until one of them fell off the train and got killed. She just happened to be the Circuit Judge's wife. He took it hard and tried to press charges but the women all got together and helped him through the grief. I let him stay at the MT Building for awhile. The girls there gave him a whole new perspective and a new mellow attitude. There were a lot less hangings in the Parker area after that.

Getting back to the bonfire. One of the more exuberant partygoers decided there was too much whiskey going to waste sitting on a store shelf when it could be put to better use at the party. He rode his horse through the plate glass window in the front of the store and almost got away with the hooch if it hadn't been for the owner's two pit-bull terriers that made short work of his pant legs. You have never seen one man sober up faster in his life. The last time I saw him he was headed for the mill pond. I didn't have the heart to tell him how good those dogs could swim.

I felt bad for Marge, the owner of the store and offered to replace the window. Getting the horse untangled from the window frame was another story altogether. Out of this minor disaster came a turn of good luck. Marge and I became close friends. From then on, if something new came into her store, I was the first to know about it.

The MT Building was a disaster. We tore up this and scraped up that and finally found the core of the building to be intact. The military had built just about everything to such incredibly heavy duty standards you would think nuclear war had already been invented. I think they were expecting an attack because the lower walls were three feet thick and the basement was carved out of solid granite.

We found several old boarded up escape tunnels going hundreds of feet in three different directions. We made great use of those tunnels when an unexpected wife would show up at the brothel with a shotgun or a so-called self-professed dignitary wanted to not be seen coming in the front door. Those tunnels got a lot of use and worked pretty well except for the time the bear got loose in there; ah… but that's another story.

The walls above ground were built from logs over two feet thick. The building had its own spring-fed water system with a natural waterfall that runs down the back of the building. Sometime after the original building was finished, a waterwheel was built to supply electricity that still works today.

We also found that a lot of former owners had really mickey moused (sorry Walt, it's just a construction term) a lot of things. We even found one of the former owners wives (we think?) plastered in a wall behind a planter. I am really glad I had the old man's money because it was going to take a lot more than a dream to fix this one up. I'll spare you the construction details.

Needless to say, a lot of townspeople made some pretty healthy paychecks. I got most of it back when the gambling hall opened.

One of the local organizations tried to keep us from opening, but the Mayor, a good upstanding citizen with ten kids, didn't need much coaxing. He was given a free preview of the brothel and a lifetime pass to the liquor cabinet. It's amazing how much service you can get from a bureaucrat when you have photos of him passed out in bed with six naked women none of which are his wife.

Getting back to this journal I am supposed to be keeping. I haven't figured any way out of it, so I guess I'll just have to plunge headlong into it.

Sometimes I think God has a little mean streak. He wants someone like me to take over the job of town historian along with my regular duties as the Guardian Angel. I'm not real great with paperwork and have never been a writer except for that time Mary Beth Walker broke my heart in several pieces, leaving me commode hugging drunk, spewing some of the most pathetic poetry you ever heard in your life. Thank Heaven nobody read it before I burned it.

Chapter Five

Which Curtains Go Better
With My Eyes?

After some healthy encouragement from God in the form of an E-mail, I arrived at the MT Building early Saturday night for my first attempt at finding recent historical moments for God's journal project.

The building I call home in the twenty-first century is a lot different than the one I rebuilt back in the 1890s and being an angel living here is a lot different than being a human. My life as an angel is really a lot more fun. I can only compare it being older and more mature if that means anything to whoever is reading this. I have more confidence and life experience than I did as a kid. As an angel I get to use the equivalent of eons of time and incredibly good resources. (Sorry I can't divulge much more.) Rest assured…life is good.

The building has a variety of levels each with its own *motif*, and has been transformed into a *gathering oasis for people of all ages*. Alcohol is not served, nor is smoking allowed within 50 feet. Fire code you know.

The last owners were a gay vegan couple who read a library full of design books and fought over which paint color would "go better with my eyes!" Apparently they had spent a lot of time in Florida and wanted to bring a little of Miami with them. Consequently there are a lot of bright pastel rugs and enough tropical plants to make Hawaii jealous.

On the bottom floor is a stage with a dance floor where sometimes plays are performed. In the outer levels, former bunk rooms were converted to classes on everything from crafts to computers. There are little gift shops keeping up the tradition of buying things from China and claiming to have made them with your own two hands; signed of course by a fourth generation Parkerite of possible Native-American heritage.

In one room there is a museum that has a few pictures of me and some of the long-dead townspeople in our natural element. I've been instrumental in coming up with some of these artifacts and left them in places where they could be found.

The old pipe organ is still there and thanks to several interested angels it stays in perfect working order. Jonathon had it given Universal Treasure status so it has to be celestially maintained.

I love being an angel. Every once in a while I pick out a new body and go down for a little practice on the keys.

I get a kick out of showing up as an eight year old kid who can play songs from the 1890s like a professional. The only trouble I have is explaining why my parents are not there. Sometimes I talk a couple of other angels into going along for the ride. Before anyone gets suspicious, I just sneak around the corner and come back as someone else. You would like being an angel!

I still love the sound of those old pipes (and the applause). Jonathon comes by now and then to share new songs he writes and makes sure everything still works properly. He claims to have been the inspiration for a little group called the Beatles and having met John Lennon and George Harrison on the Other Side, I think he may not be too far off his rocker. As an angel he looks an awful like Lennon.

Chapter Six

Do You Mind If I Wear
My Parachute to Dinner?

Saturday nights in mid-July have been real popular for the MT Building. Tonight should be no exception. The weather has been a little warmer and there are a lot of tourists in town. I guess I'll start writing in the journal as I listen in on that couple hugging on the deck by the railing as they look over the cliff. Their names are Misty and Manny Williams, newlyweds.

They were laughing and making small talk about how great it is to be on vacation. I thought they were hikers from the looks of their backpacks. I was getting a little bored until suddenly they both climbed up on the rail and jumped. I ran over and looked down expecting the worst.

Out of the blue, a pair of canopies opened. I saw a guy with a video camera come out from behind a tree. After the pictures made the evening news nationwide, it started a rash of people sneaking into the MT with parachutes and video cameras. That's one way to get out of paying your check!

Later on the Other Side... I met a couple of jumpers whose parachutes didn't open until they hit the *Other Side*. They thought death was "cool." "Amazing light tunnel dude!"

Now these knuckleheads can jump all they want with no danger since they are already dead. Somehow it takes the fun out of it knowing you are no longer defying death. Most of these types end up going back to Earth as a bird, an airline pilot or a flying insect. There is one right now buzzing around my ear.

I looked around for my next story and found two women sitting in the corner rolling silverware for the night's dinner crowd. The place has great food and an amazing variety of live entertainment. The MT Building has become a center for aspiring actors, musicians, writers and artists of all ages. It even caters to talent scouts from all the big production companies on a regular basis.

Parker Town is going *upscale*.

Some people think that is a good thing, others can't cope with change. They clash every month at the city council meeting. I think big money is winning but at least the ecologists have some control over the type of construction that can be allowed in the Parker Town limits. The ecologists were here first and established some very strict environmental laws. I have been in the middle of that one. I speak through a man named Clyde who is very quiet the rest of the time. They can't believe it's the same person when he gets up in front of the council. He did all the study. I just supply the nerve and a passionate voice. It's a lot of fun and helps protect what we have all grown to love.

Chapter Seven

Help! My Husband is
Getting Really Weird

I listened in on the two waitresses rolling silverware into cloth napkins........

"I hate rolling silverware. I am really an *actress* you know," said the younger of the two as she fluttered her eyelashes.

"Well, let's see how good you are. Act as if you *like* rolling silverware." said the older one as they both laughed. "It sure beats staying home with that jerk I married."

"Doesn't he treat you nice?" asked the younger one with concern.

"The biggest night of his life was when one of his buddies gave him an old TV and a DVD player for the garage. They scrounged up a dirty old couch, a beat-up refrigerator and a second hand beer tap. I didn't see either one of them for six months. The worst day of my life was when his buddy got mad and took it all back. Now my husband is moping around the house like a whipped puppy and keeps changing channels right in the middle of my cop shows," she snickered. "I figured it would be better to get a job at night than have to look at taped reruns of last year's hockey finals."

"I have been having boyfriend troubles too," said the younger girl sadly.

"Really? A pretty girl like you?"

"Thanks, I just wish the boys thought that too. They never seem to notice, no matter what I do. I even dyed my hair blonde. All I got was a *gee you sure looked better as a brunette.*"

"I know the feeling. I was trying to spice things up, so I pranced right up to the front door naked. My husband showed up with his boss and two of his buddies. All he said was, 'when's dinner?' and 'ain't you getting a little cold running around like that?' I fixed them. I served dinner naked. It's amazing how nonchalant three guys can be when they can't look you in the eye."

"You're kidding aren't you?" said the young girls slightly appalled.

"Yeah, actually it was my fault. I forgot he had been planning this night for a couple of weeks. I'd been watching too many soap operas and started thinking my life was just like Jennifer on *As the World Burns*. I had to quit watching that junk. It was really making me crazy."

"Me too. I was having weird dreams about a scruffy handsome man in a leather coat sneaking into my room and dragging me off to Egypt. The worst of it was; I was starting to like the idea," the young girl snickered as she turned beet red.

"Hmm, that does sound kind'a fun! You know, TV really has a lot of influence. You wouldn't believe what has happened to my husband lately. We've been married for almost 29 years and even though I called him a jerk, it's not really true. I love the big lug! I just have to get away from him for awhile to appreciate him. But get this! It was trash day and I looked out by the curb in front of the house and the beer cooler is being carried off by the garbage man. There must have been some beer left in it because it looked heavy when the driver put it in the front seat of the truck. He probably thought it was his Christmas bonus. My husband isn't really much of a drinker anyway but it was his pride and joy just to have it when his buddies came over. I also noticed a box marked *satellite dish*. We've only had three channels in this town since forever and two of them are the same. I knew something was up when he kept getting a lot *friendlier*, if you know what I mean, like at night when I got off work. I knew something was up so I told him I was going to work and sneaked around the garage and peeked in the back window. You are not going to believe it!" laughed the older woman as she tried to describe a fifty year man in bright orange spandex trunks with a lot of hair pouring out of a sleeveless skin-tight tank top. "He was jumping around singing, *It's My Party and I'll Cry If Want To,* with tears running down his face… Just him and Richard

Simmons. Are you ready for that?" laughed the older woman.

"Are you kidding? You mean that big guy with the beard that picked you up the other night? So what do you think of all this?" laughed the younger girl slightly embarrassed and thinking she'll never be able to face this woman's husband again without cracking up.

"Well, at first I thought maybe he'd gone off his rocker, literally. He's over fifty and raised five kids. Before this happened, I was fully expecting to come home one day and find him dead from heart failure on the couch with a disk of *Sports Most Nauseating Moments* running on the DVD and a half empty bag of barbecue chips spilled out on the floor. Now I don't know what to think. Besides it's getting worse. He's starting to order stuff off the TV Home Shopper. The first thing to arrive was the Juice Man Juicer. He's been ordering carrots by the fifty pound bag and growing his own parsley in the window box in the kitchen. He's lost over forty pounds and I don't know what to do. I'm afraid he'll get pretty and not want me anymore. We spent last Saturday night washing the gray out of his hair, shaving his back and bleaching his teeth!"

"You *have* been watching too many soaps."

"Now he's buying gold chains from the Jewelry Net and I actually caught him throwing away his favorite old beat-up jeans. He even threw his Harley-Davidson ball cap into the fireplace. I have been trying to throw out that ratty junk for years and he kept finding 'em and bringing 'em back. I think there may even be a pair of *Dockers and a Tommy Bahama shirt* on order. What the heck I am I going to do?" said the older woman, obviously distraught.

"Gee, it sounds good to me," giggled the young girl.

"I guess so. Maybe he'll let me have that tummy tuck and boob lift I been bugging him about."

Chapter Eight

A Woman Named Petunia is
Lowering the Crime Rate

I can't figure out what God wants with this stuff but orders are orders and the "grand purpose" must be appeased.

I think I'm getting the hang of this lap-top. Too bad it's been set so I can't access the games during working hours. Do you think someone up there doesn't trust me? Actually I'm getting kind of a kick out of this project, now that I've got it started. It's still early. Guess I'll pop into a body and go over and play the pipe organ while the rest of the dinner crew is setting up for the evening. It is going to be a special night. The house-band will be here to do a sound check in half an hour. Thirty-five, 4th and 5th graders are coming to watch the "vaudeville show" and will be arriving soon by bus. You can feel the calm before the storm.

I better explain what has happened. A new manager has taken over the MT Building. A genuine expert in the non-profit field, she is bubbling over with great ideas.

Petunia used to run a place in Boulder, Colorado that was a huge hit. But the owner started taking credit for her work giving her less and less room for creativity, not to mention more hours and less pay.

One day she just hopped in her VW microbus with her two scruffy dogs, a bird, and a pet lizard. She kept driving until she ran out of road. The van is parked around the back with a blown engine. She was towed into town and has no intention of getting it fixed. She calls it her "summer condo" and uses it to take naps every afternoon between 1 and 3. Says she learned to take a *siesta* in Mexico and refuses to break the tradition. Sounds good to me. I've been doing it for years and didn't know there was a name for it.

The first thing she did was toss out all the old potted plants and replaced them with fresh new ones. She rebuilt the stage and put in a new lighting and sound system. She planted a garden in the back and outfitted the bar for juices and health foods. The alcohol was removed from the premises with a "goodbye ceremony" and the smokers are now asked to leave town quietly so "there won't be a problem." We have had people light up at eleven thousand feet and pass out cold on the sidewalk. I suggested we put up warning signs by the information office. One of our less enthusiastic locals stole the sign because he likes to take videos of tourists passing out and uploading them to YouTube. Whatever!

"I want families to come here and feel welcome. This place is for kids too!" she proclaimed as she ripped out walls and put in an art studio for all ages with a bank of computers to work with graphics and another room for more dirty endeavors such as woodworking, oil painting and sculpture. This building is so huge that most of the projects or performances don't even overlap.

The funny thing is, she has done it all on a shoestring. The business is a non-profit connected to some *save the something or other*. The support she has received from the locals has been really great. Especially when she started the daycare center for all ages. You can drop off the kids and Grandpa too. (The MT will even take care of your pets "if they behave.")

The sheriff said the crime has gone down since this woman came to town. Of course, at this time, the only crime was a few delinquent fishing licenses and a string of poorly done graffiti performed by a 12 year old who just moved here from LA. Petunia caught him by the throat one night and now has him painting a mural on the side of the market next to the MT Building. She explained to him that "artists get paid for their work and taggers go to jail. You choose which title you want to be known by!" Luckily a local professional artist took the kid under his wing and made sure the mural got finished without any trouble or profanity. The hardware store keeps spray cans of paint under lock and key and all is well in Parker Town.

Tonight Petunia is running around with a clipboard full of stuff to catch up on, ordering the crew to do this, that and the other. Everyone loves her because she has such a great smile and once they realized that she really *does* know what she's talking about, they quit questioning her authority and jump right in and help. She's like a "Little Red Hen" at 5 foot 2, 110 pounds, buzzing around with her cell-phone in one hand and a clip-board in the other. She's somewhere around 27 and never been married. "Just couldn't see being tied down."

I sneaked into her van and read her diary once. Okay! So it wasn't ethical! It's one of the perks of being an angel. We get to do stuff like that if it's for someone's good, (justifying *how* good can be hard sometimes. Lucky for me God gets a good laugh at my pathetic excuses and has a soft-spot for a good-intentioned scoundrel).

Petunia and I hadn't met on the Other Side but I heard about her before she came to Earth. She was an angel too and just as sneaky. I want to write about her but she keeps a good lid on her privacy. I just wish she would open up. Even her diary didn't give away the real person. It mostly talked about others. She has a good heart and loves the kids who come to her for jobs and tries to help as many as she can.

Everyone loves Petunia after they get to know her and she often finds herself fending off the local boys. She's always polite but leaves them standing there talking to themselves if they get too pushy.

I'll get back to our lovely manager whose real name, by the way, is Elaine, but her friends nicknamed her "Petunia" because she is always planting flowers everywhere. She liked it better than plain Elaine and had her name changed legally to Petunia; much to the chagrin of her mother whose name is also Elaine. Her father had wanted to name her Deloris but still calls her Punkin.

Right now I need a break. I think I'll go fire up the pipes, the organ that is. You can go get something warm to drink and I'll be back in a bit. Put on a little soft music and let your eyes rest.

Chapter Nine

But Do They Take Requests?

So did you go get something warm to drink or did you just continue on? Shame on you. Go pamper yourself. This story is not so important that your comforts have to be denied.

Okay. Feeling better? I'm glad for you. Besides it gave me a few minutes to think.

Lately I've been bringing Jonathon with me. We sit at the pipe organ and play the old tunes in our new young bodies. He likes to look about thirty, rugged and handsome, a kind of Harrison Ford look-alike. When I first met him he was all bent over, somewhere in his eighties, bald with a huge nose. Just think of Jimmy Durante and you had Jonathon.

"Hey, this time I can choose what I look like!" he laughs as he gently runs his fingers over the keys. "I still can't get enough. It's really the finest instrument I've ever played on this Earth," he said as he wiped a tear from his eye. "Listen to the tone of those pipes! Awesome!"

"I heard God has one over on that little green planet that makes this one look like child's play but He won't let too many angels near it." I said.

"I got to hear it one time. Unbelievable!! Let me tell you. You should hear the music God's band plays!" said Jonathon with a smile.

"But do they take requests?" I laughed.

Chapter Ten

I Knew There Was a Reason
For All Those Music Lessons

It was still early in the evening. The theatre that houses the pipe organ hadn't opened yet. I was in a musical mood so I sat down and played a couple of songs I had written. I felt someone watching from behind and turned to see a little Mexican boy about seven years old standing there with a dreamy look on his face.

"You play pretty good Senor. Could you teach me?" he asked with bright-eyed enthusiasm.

"Sure. Sit right up here and place your hands like this," I instructed.

The look in his eye reminded me of myself so many years ago. He proceeded to play a simple Latin song that was beautifully festive. Even with the mistakes you could tell the kid had talent and natural rhythm. I filled in the bass parts because he couldn't reach the pedals. We both ended up cracking up by the end of the song. It's moments like these that make all those hours of practice worth it.

"I better get back to the computer room. My mother is probably looking for me. Can we do this again?" he asked with a look of real hope.

"Are you kidding? I wouldn't miss it for the world. Next time, bring your mother and we'll set up a schedule for lessons. Here's my phone number. The only thing you will have to bring is a polishing cloth to help me get the dust off the pipes."

"Gracias Senor! Muchas gracias!" he laughed as he ran to tell his mother, almost knocking over Petunia as she rounded the corner.

Petunia was watering her flowers and humming a little tune when I made another attempt to find out something about her to enter into the journal.

She was talking to one of the guys who volunteered to teach computers. I think he has a little crush on her, but who wouldn't? Let's listen in. I'm in invisible mode and ready to write:

"I'm really enjoying my work with the kids," said Tim looking a bit awkward.

"They sure can be a handful, but they seem to be taking to you. What's on your agenda for this week?" asked Petunia who always looks confident.

"We are going to start a mystery story. Each of us will take a part and not tell anyone. We'll put it all together at the end of the week. We're going to use the plaque in the lobby for inspiration."

I liked this guy already.

"The one about the original owner who got shot?" asked Petunia.

"Yeah. What do you think?" said Tim hopefully.

"Sounds good to me. I can help. I found some old newspapers with the story of his death in it just the other day when I was cleaning out one of the old storage bins in the attic. Come by later and I'll get them for you."

"Great, thanks. That'll be a big help!" said Tim shyly.

I was hoping for a nice juicy story out of Petunia but she hardly ever talks about herself. This may be more difficult than I thought. I'm ready for dinner. I'll come back a little later when the place gets hopping.

Chapter Eleven

Interchangeable Bodies
What a Great Idea!

The food here is great! I came to dinner in a great big fat guy body and ordered half the menu. Another angel perk.

It was about 7:30 and the band was getting set up in the main hall. The dinner crowd was building up and the place was getting noisy. I was starting to get more excited about my assignment.

I shed the big body just before indigestion set in, shifted into invisible mode and hovered just high enough off the floor to not wince every time a waitress went by with a tray. I will probably never get used to people being able to walk right through me like that. I'll tell you what though, it's really fun to walk through walls, fall over cliffs and get run over by cars without getting hurt. But sometimes when I take on a new body I forget what mode I'm in and get the funniest looks as I run into the door. The bodies we use have feeling and sometime it really hurts. A quick reminder as to how you humans feel all the time. It's really embarrassing when I think I'm invisible and I'm not, especially when I get an itch. We'll talk about that some other time.

I'm perched in the air above the crowd looking around for my next story.... I see a Rolls-Royce pull up in the drive. Out steps a fifty year old confident man of obvious wealth and a woman who looks highly capable of taking it away from him. Of course this is my analytical first-sight observation which usually turns out to be completely wrong.

Yes! I was right about being wrong. They entered the room as if they owned the place and with a well-placed ten-dollar bill settled into the best seats available, in a corner with a view, looking out over the cliff. They sat looking dreamy-eyed at each other and complained out-loud because alcohol is not served no matter how much money you flash around.

The town drunk (don't laugh, every town has at least one official town drunk) just happened to be sitting within earshot and offered them a drink of some kind of solvent he had in a paper sack. They both turned up their noses and passed looks of disgust along with rolling eyes and a slight snicker.

The Town Drunk was obviously used to this by now and it did not deter him a bit from offering to rescue them from lack of drink by going to the local liquor store and picking up a bottle… at a small carrying fee of course.

The big shot flipped him a hundred-dollar bill and named some upscale bubbly that Oscar had never heard of, let alone pronounce. He said "gotcha covered!" and disappeared for half an hour. Oscar arrived back with a gallon of *Thunderbird* that looked to have about a third gone and almost dropped it as he plunked it down on their table.

Eagle eyes Petunia spotted this out of the corner of her eye and immediately swept the bottle away from the surprised couple and threw the drunk out the door, all in one quick sweep. She didn't even explain her actions, just went about her business lighting candles as if nothing had happened.

I like Petunia. She reminds me of Kathryn Hepburn with bigger boobs. Same attitude. Nothing fazes her. I've got to figure out how to get her to talk about herself.

Meanwhile, back to the couple. By now the cell phone in his pocket has gone off and got the attention of the whole place with some heavy-metal guitar-based ring-tone. He's had it glued to his ear for the last fifteen minutes and the lady is looking bored. He's trying to impress her with his business prowess.

I looked at the Rolls and found out it belongs to a rental company in Beverly Hills. The guy on the other end of the phone is his old roommate from college. It looks like our boy is a phony. I wonder what he hopes to gain from this one. He hangs up the phone and looks smug. Our elegant lady looks away but you could tell she is slightly impressed in spite of herself. She knows something is up but just can't put her finger on it. She ransacked the glove compartment when he went into a store for a pack of cigars and knows the car is rented but has decided to ride out the fantasy anyway. *It's not every day when a dog groomer from Rawlins Wyoming gets to look like a million...* He had picked her up on a Denver street when, on a whim, she had rented a Corvette for the day. So who was fooling who anyway?

A Short Pause for Communication

I sent in an E-mail to God and just got a return.
I wrote:

> *Dear God,*
>
> *I am starting to get a kick out of this*
> *assignment. Any new requests?*
>
> *Love, Griffin*

It came back:

> *Dear Griffin,*
>
> *Could you give us a little more background*
> *on Parker Town when you were alive? This*
> *doesn't have to be written all in one night.*
> *Take your time and have fun.*
>
> *With Love Always, Big Daddy*

God has an incredible sense of humor and wants all of us to enjoy whatever we are doing to the utmost. We are all like a bunch of puppies in the eyes of God and His Wife. They love to watch us having a good time. It's too bad we take so many things serious. I guess it's hard to see the big picture when your garbage disposal is backed up, the electric bill comes due and the kid needs braces just as the car is breaking down a week after the warranty ran out.

I was feeling like I could stretch out a little now that this book didn't have to be written all in one night. This was just crossing my mind when another E-mail dropped in. It said:

Dear Griffin

If you take too long you'll miss something really cool that I have planned.

Love, from the Top.

Another paradox! Hurry up and wait! But if God has something "really cool" in mind, it must be. I had better get back to work.

Mark Griffin

Chapter Twelve

A Road Trip Just Wouldn't Be Right Without a Breakdown

The MT Building is starting to fill up. Being a Saturday night, people come from little towns scattered all over the mountains, also from the narrow-gauge train that chugs up out of the valley. It looks like it's going to be a busy night. The waiters and waitresses are zipping around trying to keep up. I am in invisible mode again and looking for my next story. A family of seven just walked in the door. Let's listen in.

"Well! If you hadn't had to take so much junk with us we wouldn't be in this predicament!" yelled the wife whose name was Barbara.

"Okay, Okay! Can we at least stop fighting long enough to get something cold to drink. Walking that last two miles just about exhausted me," replied the sweaty husband as he looked around for a table.

"How many?" asked the hostess. "Well there were seven just a minute ago. Where the hell is Jamie?"

"She had to go to the bathroom and so do we," cried the rest of the kids ranging from five to thirteen.

"Okay, but don't take forever. And all of you wash your hands," yelled the mother. "We'll get a table and then I'm headed that way too. Miss! Can you get us a gallon or two of iced tea?"

"I sure can!" said the waitress with a big smile. "Right away."

I thought, this ought to be good. They are obviously on a somewhat misguided vacation. Something must have happened to the car. I'll look outside. Must be the mini-van behind ol' Jake's tow-truck. He's headed this way.

I've known Jake for a long time. He's in his late nineties but looks to be seventy, a scruffy old German with a leathery face and a heart of gold. I've seen him pull people out of the snow at four in the morning without a complaint. He's one of those plain old tough guys who has worked hard all his life and wouldn't trade what he does for anything. Actually he makes really good money and enjoys the fact that when he is needed he is *really* needed. He prides himself on being honest and has gone out of his way to be fair, sometimes to his own detriment.

I remember the time a lady from Chicago got side-tracked and ended up on one of our mountain roads that eventually leads to nowhere. She was desperate and it was getting dark. Luckily she had a cell phone. He was out there half the night trying to follow her desperate but creative description of just exactly where she located. It turned out she was only about a half mile from Jake's house as the crow flies but about 10 miles by dirt road.

Am I getting off-track? What about the family you ask? Sorry. I have always been easily distracted.

Nowadays they call it *Attention Deficit Disorder*; or *ADD*. We used to call it daydreaming.

Anyway enough already. This is what I could find out. This is the first vacation the whole family has had in several years. Both parents work and could never get time off at the same time. The husband may not have a job when they get back and has spent the whole time worrying about it, out loud. He spent the last two hours on his cell-phone. His wife had to drive and the kids are about to disown him. It's really too bad because he's a nice guy who loves his family so much that he doesn't know how to let the world go and just be.

The cellular phone just went over the cliff and bounced off several rocks. It's swinging from the strap on a tree branch about five hundred feet below. "There! Now I don't want to hear one more word about your job or anything else connected to home until we're pulling into the driveway in two weeks!" screamed the wife as she tried to hold back the tears. "We're going to have a good time if it kills us!"

"But Honey......"

"No buts! I have spoken!" she exclaimed as she started to laugh.

"A round of cheeseburgers for all of us!" cried the father as he realized just how tense he had been. "I sure love that woman," he thought as he looked over at her and the kids. "The car should be ready by morning and we're off to see the Grand Canyon."

Well as far as I know they lived happily ever after except for a massive case of indigestion from eating everything on the menu. This may not sound like much of an in depth report but it's not meant to be a biography, just small moments in the lives of strangers that make us all feel as if we really are interconnected somehow. Smidgens of life that are not exactly earthshaking, that find a place in your heart and make the tear ducts itch a little. Was that a cute way of describing this book or just a bunch of flowery fluff to fill space? You choose.

So much for sentimental drivel you say. What about the tow truck driver? Now that guy looks like stories are just crawling out his ears. As a matter of fact he has a secret that I retrieved from a friend of his here on *this side*, one Jake will probably take to his grave.

Jake the tow truck driver is one of those people who just oozes strength, he has a very tough exterior but inside he knows the reality of fear. When Jake, which is not his real name was a boy in Germany the war was raging. Hitler was seen as a new messiah and his father and brother were all gung-ho as they showed off their new uniforms to the people in the little town. They both took off to fight for the German Army along with most of the other able-bodied men in the town.

They were given a heroes send-off as they puffed out their chests and rode off on the train to glory. His father was the first to come home in a government issue box with a sincere "thank you" from the Furor himself. His brother's ID card, found in a charred wallet, were all that could be salvaged after he tried to escape the Allied bombings only fifty miles from Jake's hometown. The body was blown to bits. His mother was never the same.

At the ripe old age of thirteen Jake was the man of the family. He did his best to comfort his mother but knew deep down that no words would ever be the right ones. That was the year the war ended, but not before soldiers forced him from his home to serve too. He was big for his age and they didn't believe that he was only thirteen. He never saw his mother or sister again. He was placed in a concentration camp as a guard and hated every minute.

The atrocities that Jake witnessed turned his stomach as he learned first-hand the cruelties of man against man. He swore if he ever got out of this alive he would treat all people equal and go out of his way to help anyone in need.

He escaped just as the American forces entered the camp and with the help of a friend who was educated in the USA, worked their way out of Germany on every back road they could find. He learned English from the American prisoners and discovered he had a profound memory. Some even called it photographic. Jake and his friend worked on their accents until they sounded like typical blonde, blue-eyed boys from California. They fooled enough people to pass as Americans.

As they traveled on foot, scared, worn out, hungry, dirty and cold, they saw first-hand the devastation of war and swore a pact with each other to never be a part of such a horrible thing again.

The very next day his friend stepped on a forgotten land mine and left Jake alone in the world. Scared and hungry he decided then and there to go to America. He had made friends with many of the Americans in the camp and found them to be to his liking. It left a huge impact on him when several of the prisoners were shot trying to escape. Luckily he was not on duty or he would have had to do his part as a soldier. He was sick for several weeks afterword.

As he traveled, Jake broke into libraries at night and read everything he could about the land of promise.

His luck changed when a sailor that looked like him was killed in a bar fight where Jake was washing dishes. In the midst of the chaos, he grabbed the sailor's dog tags and orders from his coat pocket. He found his way to the ship and with more nerve than he thought he could stand; he went on board as Seaman First Class, Jake Applegate.

He got a small reprimand for being out of uniform but in the middle of all the celebration of a world war coming to an end no one noticed one more sailor quietly minding his own business. He even collected the dead man's pay. It wasn't much, but it gave him an identity and a start.

He hitched rides on freight trains and traveled all over the United States doing odd jobs. Nights he spent in the libraries and book stores learning all he could about everything in the world. His thirst for knowledge was insatiable.

You may think this was the big secret. Not so. The big secret was that he had worked his way to Wall Street and with his photographic mind made over 10 million dollars on the stock exchange. He took the money and ran, bought himself a modest cabin and a second hand tow truck in a little mountain town and feels good about himself. He gives anonymously to children's research and tows the people he likes for free. He liked the young couple with their five kids. There will be a nice surprise in the glove compartment from an old man who has seen it all. The job the father was so worried about won't be necessary in his new business and Jake has adopted another loving family. He will get cards, letters and phone calls from a grateful family until the day he passes.

I have never been through a war and I don't really have the close point of view that Jake had but I know I would never want to have anything to do with it. I was traveling around on the Heaven side and found myself at a receiving station for victims of a war that was going on a few years after I had left the Earth. I talked to a few of the new arrivals. They were surprised to wake up on this side but not too surprised considering the circumstances they had just left. Most said they would miss their loved ones and felt a deep sorrow for what had gone on. Many were still angry until they realized the enemy was also present, waking up by their sides. Some of these people didn't even know what they were fighting about and became good friends. Others are still enemies and will go through eternity carrying this burden. It usually eats at them until they choose to go back and fight another war on another planet. These spirits will continue this until they hit bottom and find that love and forgiveness are the only truths that can save them from their own private hell. Everyone has to learn at their own pace and God has all the time in the world.

This side is very much like being on Earth. We are free to choose how we want to live and who we live it with. Personally, I am thankful for this little town and it's ever changing, ever the same lifestyle. It's my home and my little bit of Heaven.

Chapter Thirteen

You Don't Look a
Day Over a Hundred and Ten

I was standing by the entrance to the old MT Building when a lady in one of those fancy new electric wheel chairs burst through the door. A big grin across her face, a loud "Howw...deeee!" and everyone knew ol' Jessie had arrived. She raced around the dining room chasing the waitresses and hollering, "Out of the way you sinners... I'm a'comin' through!" She did a couple loops around the room and screeched to a stop at the hostess station.

"Are you gonna find me a table or do I have to go find it myself?" she hollered as she headed for her favorite spot. The one with a view.

One of her grand entrances will always crack a smile on some folks and totally offend some others. She just laughs and grabs the nearest kids. She fills their heads with yarns that keep them spellbound on the edge of their chairs. The parents love her in spite of themselves.

"I have stories I haven't even made up yet!" she would say as she gives the kids a big warm smile and if they were within reach, a big hug and a "smooch."

She always carries funny things in her pockets. The kids that know her all call her "Granny." The local grouches call her "that crazy old broad." There usually isn't a frown within earshot when she gets through. She refuses to allow anyone to be crabby no matter how hard they try.

I have really come to look forward to seeing her. She claims to be 123 years old and has the energy of a 50 year-old although lately you can tell it's running out. I told her she didn't look a day over a hundred and ten. I asked God if it would be all right if I was the angel that gets to greet her when she passes over and darned if He didn't say "yes."

I like to take on a young man's body that looks a lot like someone she had a crush on in high school every once in a while and go visit her at her home. She can't remember where we met but loves to have company. I can talk to her by the hour. She doesn't know it but we share a lot of the same memories. I just tell her it was a story my Grandpa Walter told me.

I am also allowed to talk to her in her dreams. We have been close friends for quite a while. She has so much love for life and especially for kids that sometimes I think she is going to burst. She'll make a terrific angel someday. She is one of those rare souls that I feel it has been a privilege to know. It is an honor to tell her story. I hardly know where to begin. A person like her has led such a full life. Someday maybe I'll write her life's story but for now I have to keep it brief.

Chapter Fourteen

The Preacher Didn't Like Her
So She Married Him

J essie Ann Jones first came to Parker Town somewhere around 1890. She was the wildest rootin,' tootinest, horsebreakinest, crazy, wild woman anyone had ever seen. On her first day the local preacher tried to have her thrown out of town.

"She's loud and dresses peculiar!" he roared.

She fixed him. She married him the following summer. *Took the starch right out of his collar.*

At the time of this writing they have 14 kids, 54 grandkids and 16 great-grandkids, with 3 on the way.

The funny thing was, his name was Jones too, no relation, so she didn't even have to change her name.

Jessie was always there whenever anyone needed anything. No job was too big or too small. She took over the birthing of babies when Doctor Henry was out of town and brought a lot of animals into the world too. Her specialty was horses. No one ever lived that loved horses more than Jessie. The only reason she has been confined to a wheel chair; she fell off her horse at the age of 122 and broke her hip. She says, "I'll be back on that ol' nag by the middle of summer. Just you wait and see!" What she meant by that was, she would lead the parade at the town rodeo on the 4th of July just like she had for as long as anyone could remember.

In the meantime she has been seen terrorizing the tourists as they get off the train, selling little trinkets she makes in her kitchen. She doesn't need the money, just likes the attention. She won't take no for an answer and sells an amazing amount of stuff. She donates the money to a children's hospital.

The most famous story that everyone tells about Jessie was the night she found the owner of the MT Building shot to death in his bed. Yes, that was me.

She caught the lady red-handed and wrestled her to the ground as she tried to escape. It was early in the morning and still dark. Jessie was out for her usual morning walk before breakfast. She was one of those people who can only sleep a few hours a night and then she's rarin' to go.

She heard the gunshot and was almost knocked down by the lady who landed on the ground next to her. The woman had jumped off the second floor balcony and had a crazy look in her eye.

By this time both of them were so full of adrenaline that it took four cowboys and the sheriff to separate them.

Jessie was a hero after that and loved to tell anyone who would listen how it all came about. Of course over the years the story got bigger and bigger. The tale she tells the kids today is so overblown you'd think she was Wonder Woman saving the entire world from evil. It's all right with me. I'm a sucker for a good story.

Chapter Fifteen
Nobody Appreciates My Sense of Fashion

The town is getting ready for the annual Bluegrass Festival and the old MT Building is buzzing. The MT is one of the sponsors this year and Petunia is a basket case. She has been calling all over the country trying to get a hold of some name acts that just might have a weekend free. She is trying to upgrade the show. People were getting tired of the same old acts year after year. The band she had on contract cancelled due to a drug overdose. It's tough this late in the season to find bands that are not already booked a year in advance. She really wants to make this a special event and has put just about every waking moment into it.

Like most bluegrass festivals there are always little jam sessions on every corner all night. She's been practicing her autoharp and has been digging out some old tunes she used to play with a group in Boulder. I just wish she would let loose a little bit. I still can't get her to talk about herself even if my life depended on it.

Parker Town, although isolated, is not on another planet. It has satellite TV service, a new and used car dealership. The hardware store and grocery/dry-goods emporium are still owned by the local families. The town council has held to a policy of not allowing fast food franchises and big-box stores but a tattooed, moose-haired punk rocker named Spike got through the filter known as the neighborhood watch and would have been shot at sunrise if there were no laws against it.

The locals who haven't seen MTV or been to Venice Beach are appalled by his many tattoos, his spiked green and purple hair and they hate the way he dresses with his torn black T-shirts that have skulls and biker symbols, not to mention all the pierced parts of his body, namely ears, nipples, nose, lips and God only knows what else.

He likes to live dangerously; sort of, "on the cutting edge."

In a town as western as Parker, he is getting his share of dirty looks. The local teens think he is either a dork or a god depending on who you talk to.

Spike and three of his buddies who all looked equally terrifying, left Brooklyn, New York, in an old Cadillac they bought for $600 and started their journey west. Destination: Los Angeles, the City of Angels; a new horizon and home of the most famous tattoo artists on the planet.

The first part of the adventure lasted about two and a half days of automobile hell. They experienced three flat tires, a blown alternator and ran through a lot more gas then they had money. Not to mention the air conditioner that blew out some kind of smoky stuff that gave everybody headaches.

Spike's buddies left him on the side of the road somewhere northeast of Denver with a look of determination and his thumb out. "I'll show those jerks!"

He spent all night and half the next day trying to get a ride. He even flashed a twenty dollar bill. Seems no one west of Cleveland appreciated his sense of style. Somehow, he just couldn't grasp the fact that green and purple spiked hair wasn't a fully accepted fashion in western Sterling, Colorado.

He was just about to give up when Petunia, who just can't hardly resist helping small animals and those in trouble, pulled over in the MT van and without even thinking of her own safety said, "you gonna just stand there or are you getting in?" She had been out buying supplies for the upcoming festival and took a day to visit an old friend in Sterling that gave her a dog and some other weird looking animal that no one had the nerve to ask what it was.

"Don't worry. It won't bite hard. It's old. Just don't look it in the eye," Petunia laughed as Spike crawled into the van.

Spike was so tired that he barely had the seat belt clicked when he fell instantly to sleep. Petunia woke him up just outside of Denver and asked him if he wanted to come up to Parker Town or continue down the Interstate to LA. "You'll have about an hour to decide."

He was infatuated by this "older" woman (he's 22, she's 27) who didn't try to force any opinions on him except for a 20 minute tirade about the abuse of animals. He lied when he said his black leather jacket was really vinyl. He felt compelled to find out a bit more about her and this little town she was speaking so highly of. "Who am I to argue with such a beauty? LA will always be there," he laughed. She just jammed it into first gear and hit the gas.

They arrived around midnight. Petunia gave him a cot in a backroom of the MT Building to sleep on and promised to take him on the grand tour in the morning.

He dragged himself out at the "crack of noon" and looked at his surroundings. It was a world away from the city where he had been raised. "It looks like a National Geographic photo," he thought, as he wiped the sleep from his eyes and stretched his road-weary muscles. The air was thin and he felt light-headed from the altitude, not to mention ravenously hungry. He realized how different everyone else looked when he went in search of a café and noticed how the locals were dressed. He felt like he had just been zapped onto the set of a western movie. He was up to his ears in Wrangler jeans, pearl-buttoned shirts and straw cowboy hats. Of course to someone who had gone to great lengths to make themselves look that different, he had the mistaken idea that everyone really liked his strange costume and would dress like that in a minute if they only had the nerve. He was feeling like a rock-star.

Spike walked in to the local diner with his Brooklyn swagger and pulled up a chair at the lunch-counter. He thought, "They must think I'm really cool." He sipped his coffee with the arrogance of an Oscar winner. *People will be asking for my autograph any minute*. Actually someone did, the local sheriff.

Jimmy Woods got several calls that morning from *concerned citizens*. They claimed that someone they had seen on "America's Most Wanted" was out on the street. So he headed over to the local café to check it out. Jimmy is a former hippy that cut his hair to get a cruise job in a small town with no crime. He felt a little nervous as he sat down next to Spike. "Mind if we have a few words in private?" he asked Spike.

"Okay if I bring my coffee?" replied Spike who was not feeling so high and mighty when his eyes focused on the crowd who had suddenly gone silent waiting for him to do something so they could justify tearing him to pieces. He was used to hostility in New York but had never felt any danger from it. It's all in what you get used to and this was not feeling comfortable at all. All eyes were upon him as he left the café.

They went outside and climbed into the front seat of the police car. Jimmy told him to relax.

"The same thing happened to me in 1968 when I showed up in Parker Town with hair down to my waist, an anti-war ball cap and a shirt made out of the American flag," he laughed.

"Just routine, have to check you out. Got some ID?"

"Sure," said Spike as he handed him his college student body card.

"No drivers' license?" asked Jimmy.

"I live in New York. Who drives?" Replied Spike as if everyone should know that.

"I guess this will have to do. Got any money on you?" asked Jimmy sounding official as he could without laughing.

"A couple of hundred and a credit card."

"Plan on staying long?" continued Jimmy.

"Don't know. Just got here."

"Do you know anybody here?"

He tried hard to remember her name.

"Well, I met a girl with a flower for a name. She gave me a ride and a cot for the night."

"Must be Petunia. She can't resist a stray. Did she show you her collection of animals she's been rounding up since she moved in a few months back? It's even worse now that she's got a company van," laughed Jimmy.

Jimmy kind of liked the kid with the weird hairdo as he found Spike, whose real name was Samuel Corinsky, to be free of warrants. He apologized for the inconvenience.

"Enjoy your stay in Parker Town and call if you have any problems. I run an equal opportunity police department," smiled Jimmy who was relieved to find that underneath all that weird clothing was just another normal college kid with a need to be noticed.

Spike had been there a few days and brought out the worst in the locals. The parents were terrified that he would be an influence, or even worse, try to marry one of their daughters. The shopkeepers kept calling the Sheriff's office. "Just wanted to let you know where he is." Needless to say his first couple of weeks in town stirred up a lot of nightmares and cold sweats. The hardware store said there was a run on WD-40 for the locks on the doors that hadn't been used in years.

Then Spike saved the baby...

He was down by the river playing a guitar he'd borrowed from Petunia when a young family set up a picnic upstream. He was sitting on the bank by a large boulder trying to get closer to his "inner self" when he noticed a screaming child about two years old go whipping by in the current.

"Samuel didn't even stop to think of himself," the papers reported.

Spike just jumped in, grabbed the little girl and headed for shore. He noticed she was turning blue and not breathing so he dug back into his high school CPR ("I knew watching Baywatch would come in handy sooner or later!") and performed the necessary moves. The child spit up water and took a breath just as the frantic parents came running up screaming with a look of horror in their eyes. The child's father was an ER doctor who checked the baby out and found she was no worse for wear. They forgot all about Spike's looks and spent the next half hour stuffing hot dogs and potato salad down him as they fell all over themselves trying to say "thank you" in every way imaginable.

Spike tried to keep up his tough punk look, but ended up in tears amazed at what had transpired. He became an instant local hero.

The paper did an interview that painted him as a wonderful human being. The local church decided to quit its campaign that was leading to tar and feathers and even the local librarian gave him the key to the restroom that had previously been "mysteriously unavailable."

Spike was feeling pretty good. This was the first time in his punk career that "normal" people actually talked to him. He was finding the notoriety to his liking. He decided to stay awhile if he could get work. He had been making a living in cheap clubs in New York doing a lip-sync act with two girls. Maybe it could happen here now that everyone liked him.

He talked to Petunia about it. She thought it would be a lot of fun. "I can't pay much but I can provide a room to sleep in. If you'll wash dishes at night and help cleanup in the morning you can use the theatre to rehearse."

She was surprised when he told her he would prefer to work as a computer tech since he had been taking them apart and putting them together since he was ten years old. He also had a college background in drama, sound and stage lighting which included a degree in audio. She apologized for underestimating him.

Spike went to work on the children's computers and soon had them humming. He created posters with amazing graphics advertising the MT Building. Some of the local kids helped him place them all over town reminding the townspeople that there was a place for kids and adults alike to hang out that would teach them something. He even started computer classes for adults that were soon overcrowded just by word of mouth.

The wealthy parents of the child he saved were from Palm Beach. They were still offended by his looks but felt grateful enough to give him a check for $5,000. Another $500 was offered if he would change his wardrobe. Fat chance! Spike felt as if the world was a wonderful place. Life was good after all. He set up auditions and found two girls to dress up as part of his act. Their parents made them promise in writing not to dress that way on a permanent basis or anywhere but the show. Rehearsals were going very well. The big check was more money than he had ever seen at one time. Petunia talked him into letting her "manage it" for him so he wouldn't "blow it all on something stupid."

Spike was a new man at twenty-two years old. *On top of the world.*

The big night was nearing and he had agents, promoters and newspaper coverage from Denver and as far away as LA. He spent a lot of time and money sending out texts, E-mail and faxes to everyone he could find. No promoter has ever worked harder. This was to be his moment of glory that would escalate him to stardom. He knew the gods were smiling!

His act was wild. A lip sync where he pranced, danced and flew on a cable from the ceiling with colored laser lights bouncing off the foggy smoke while he played the "air guitar" made from a loaf of French bread to several extremely hard-core punk tracks.

The MT Building was packed to the rafters. The excitement was at a fever pitch. This was going to be the biggest event of the century. He spent a week working on his costume and makeup for the girls. They rehearsed relentlessly and felt confident. Both girls threw up for two days before the performance and only slept a total of two or three hours a night. Neither girl had ever done anything like this so Spike had to continually reassure them that all would go as planned.

Ten minutes to show-time and Spike couldn't find his centerpiece, the French loaf. He was frantic. He looked everywhere. Finally ending up in the kitchen, he was horrified to find the chef had just cut it up and buttered it.

Spike went ballistic. He chased the chef around the steam table and if he hadn't slipped on a butter spill, there might have been a murder that night. He almost cried as he looked at the clock. Five minutes to show-time and no loaf. This loaf of sour-dough French was a one-of-a-kind sent in on special delivery from San Francisco; a good solid crust to withstand the rigors of air-guitar.

The adrenaline was screaming through his veins as he broke the door down on the local bakery. All he needed was one loaf. He flipped on the lights and to his chagrin all the shelves were empty, sold out. He spotted a shelf in the back of the store that was marked "DAY OLD" and there in a white paper bag was the most beautiful sight he had ever seen, a sourdough French loaf.

He grabbed it and ran for the stage just as the night deputy showed up to check out all the commotion. Seems the bakery was right next to the police station so he couldn't miss hearing the racket. He didn't see Spike as Spike dashed back to the MT Building.

The theater was going nuts. Spike had placed shills in the audience that were screaming and cheering. The girls in his act were frantic with stage-fright as it was, let alone having the star of the show missing. The act went on but he was so upset he tripped over the microphone stand knocking one of the girls off the stage. The music got out of sync and the show was a flop. The audience got hostile and left halfway through. The shills still demanded to be paid as Spike ran out into the back alley.

In between tears he gulped down a half bottle of Johnny Walker Red that someone handed him on the way out. His thoughts were based on revenge as he molded dark plots of murder and torture involving the chef.

He waited until the chef was off work and followed him home. He saw the man enter a house. He crept up and put a lighted candle on the console in his car. In his drunken state he figured the guy would see the flame and think his car was on fire; the first in a series of bad things that were forming in the mind of a madman to scare the hell out of one who had so maliciously wronged him. (Author note: Spike really didn't have it in him to actually hurt someone.)

The best-laid plans sometimes take on massive proportions when mixed with alcohol. Spike left the candle burning as he passed out in the forest behind the house. The chef who didn't look out the window went to bed and the car burned to the ground.

Spike felt so bad the next day that he turned himself in. The judge gave him 90 days and made him pay for the car. Lucky for him it was an old beat-up Dodge the chef had bought for $300. The chef claimed it was a classic and made Spike pay a thousand plus another $200 for the black spot in his driveway.

The last time I saw Spike he was hitchhiking out of town with one of the girls from the act. The townspeople all said "I told you so" to each other and went back to hating anyone who looked a little different. I feel sorry for the next punk-rocker that shows his purple and green hair in this little corner of the world.

Chapter Sixteen

Love Can Really Make
The Boys Act Weird

Joey and George just walked in. I think they're both having big-time heart palpitations for Petunia. Neither one has the nerve to let her know.

Joey is 45 years old and deep in a midlife crisis. He has been divorced for three years and is just now starting to look at younger women. He lost forty pounds at Jenny Craig and feels quite proud of himself but still feels pretty frazzled when it comes to the opposite sex. He was married twenty-two years and has three kids that are all out of school; all bent on running his life over the Internet. They all call, text, or e-mail at least once a week. He loves the attention and has enough money not to worry about the bills his kids run up.

Joey has wavy blonde hair and blue eyes, dresses better than most people around Parker Town and gets shunned by Petunia on a regular basis.

Joey and George met in a divorced men's group and really hit it off. They both left Chicago to "find a new life" and ended up in Parker Town where they started a sporting goods store. They both love to ski and dream about all the "great looking chicks they can meet on the slopes." George, 43, is divorced for the second time, dark hair with a big mustache and a high forehead. He's not as tall as Joey but makes it up with a pair of snake skin Tony Lama cowboy boots with two inch heels and a hat to match. He admits to being a drugstore cowboy, but likes the image anyway. He even bought a rodeo first prize silver buckle, but if you look close it has someone else's name engraved on it.

Joey and George are a team. They both have heartbreak and loneliness to share and a lot of money tucked away where the ex-wives can't touch it. These two are inseparable and have a heck of a time keeping regular hours in the store.

For the first year, if you wanted anything you had to call their answering service. Sometimes it took a week to get a call back. They were usually off fishing or running around in the company's 4-wheel drive Hummer chasing jack rabbits or whatever else men do in the mountains with 350 horsepower at their fingertips.

The friendship was going along great until Petunia showed up. On the outside it looked the same but hiding in the background was a shadow about to show its ugly head. Both of them fell head over heels when they first saw her but neither would admit it to the other.

Petunia acted as if she didn't notice. That drove both of them crazy. Everything probably would have worked itself out except for the fact that Joey always got first pick when they met new girls and George got the leftovers. This time George was determined not to let it happen. He didn't even stop to consider the fact that Petunia might want to be in on the decision. The best man had to win and from George's point of view he was overqualified for the job. It would take quick thought, planning and cunning to pull it off. It kept him up nights. George valued his friendship with Joey and didn't want to mess up their business relationship so whatever he did would have to be really sly.

George was watching a mouthwash commercial on the cable channel one night when the light bulb over his head came on. They were both getting ready for a double date with a couple of young tourist ladies from England. A big night was planned and the boys were shining up the boots, putting on their best clothes, and splashing on the after-shave. They were just going out the door when George allowed his hormones to take over his sense of fair play. The little devil on his shoulder had spoken.

"Hey Joey! Ya' know, we've been friends for quite a while now and only a friend would tell you. Your breath is leaving something to be desired. You better go hit the mouthwash," laughed George, as he tried to be as nonchalant and polite as possible.

"Thanks man! I'm glad you said something. I'll be right back," said Joey with a look of real concern. Joey is one of those guys who tosses out a shirt with a stain, has creases ironed into his jeans and hair that takes almost an hour to get perfect after a shower.

George laughed to himself, "this is going to be easier than I thought."

They went out on the town and had a great time but all during the night both of them were thinking about Petunia.

A few weeks went by... The ruse was already starting to work. Joey was going almost out his mind trying to clear up a case of halitosis that, in George's words, "could knock out a bull moose at thirty feet." He was eating breath mints by the hand-full, chewing gum and carrying around those little bottles of Scope and Listerine. Nothing worked. He even went to a doctor, but the doctor couldn't find a cure. He saw Joey's Porsche in the parking lot and figured even if there wasn't anything wrong he'd have to run more tests. *Mama needs a new set of boobs and hot tub to match. Sometimes it's just too easy!*

Joey was going nuts. It got so bad he refused to go out of the house and started losing weight. He spent most of his waking hours looking through medical journals and searching the Internet for clues to a condition that always seemed to disappear just before he went to the doctor. Needless to say, he wasn't doing much to wow the ladies.

In the meantime George was being ignored by Petunia because as it turns out she wasn't attracted to either one of them. "I was flattered by the competition and just trying to be polite," she laughed.

George couldn't keep it to himself and let it slip to one of the locals which immediately got back to Joey who was furious. After the initial shock wore off Joey had a new respect for George but knew he had to get revenge. Joey valued their friendship and spent nights thinking up ways to get revenge that could be pulled off without getting caught. By this time he had realized it would never happen for either one of them with Petunia so he decided to bring her in on it.

She was a "woman of the world" and had a few plans of her own. She'd show both of these knuckleheads the truth about women even if it meant stepping down to their level. She let a little time go by. Both of the boys had forgotten all about the joke. Joey is pretty easy going and finally got a big laugh out of the whole thing.

Of course, George now has a lifetime subscription to eleven gay magazines thanks to Joey. Joey likes to pull them out of the trash after George throws them out and leaves them with George's name and address at various doctor's offices around the mountain area along with George's cell-phone number. George has had to change his number three times and is still getting E-mail from some pretty friendly guys who want to share various sports with him. A side-effect was an increase in the sports equipment business that opened a whole new customer base.

Petunia finally found gentle revenge when a group of fashion models came into Parker for a photo shoot. She introduced them to Joey and George. They wanted to use the sporting goods storefront to do part of the shoot. The models drove the boys crazy calling and making plans to meet secretly. A different girl would call every little while and set up a meeting then not show up. This went on all week with lots of "professional job related" excuses and heavy apologies. Joey and George were both about to give up on the model-dating idea when a call came in from one of the prettiest of the bunch, swearing that the job was over, "could both of you guys come down to the lake where all of us girls would like to make it up to you with a night in the wild?" A good time was guaranteed for all. Joey and George were in heaven.

The full moon was just coming up on the lake when two girls actually showed up this time with smiles ear to ear and told the boys, "take off your clothes and jump in the water. It's a skinny-dipping party! You guys hop in and we'll be right there. Gotta do some girly stuff to prepare," laughed the girls as the guys stripped down and jumped in the water.

Instead of jumping into the water, the models immediately ran down to the beach. They grabbed the guy's clothes, hopped in their rent-a-car and squealed out of the parking lot. Joey and George could hear the laughter as it faded into the night. They both had a classic look of terror on their faces that looked great on the video Petunia shot from behind a tree.

They spent half the night shivering in Joey's Porsche without the keys. They finally got enough nerve to sneak home which meant they got a lot of bramble scratches from hiding in the bushes when a car came by. They had stickers in their bare feet, a possible a case of poison oak and a real bad attitude toward models from England.

They found themselves on the doorstep of Joey's house with no keys to the door. George didn't show his best side climbing through the window.

"Nice butts!" Petunia laughed as she put the finishing touches on the video with her zoom lens from outside Joey's fence. She sent them a box with their clothes in it and a copy of the video along with a note that said that she had been *so close to choosing one of them, how hard it had been to make such a choice when they both had such wonderful attributes, how jealous she was of those pretty girls, but now that she knew what womanizers they were, her heart was broken. She had no alternative but to leave town!*

Since then they have all become best friends after a pact was made to stop the jokes, at least on each other. Anyone else was fair game.

Chapter Seventeen

A Pipe-Organ is Born

A text message from God said He wanted a little more of Parker Town's history. These are some people I knew back then.

In 1875, David and Marlene Feldman were the first Jews to enter Parker Town. They brought with them skills and tenacity that will be renowned for generations. He was a watchmaker by trade and a Rabbi by religion. She specialized in having children, eight girls and five boys.

The town loved to accuse them of single-handedly starting their own synagogue. They were tough people with big hearts who wanted everything possible for their children and weren't afraid to go after it.

The long journey across the plains had left David with a few scars that he was proud of and determination that was unshakable. They both figured if they could make it that far then anything in the future would be insignificant. It wasn't true, but they liked to keep up the illusion.

I met them both the first day when I pulled into town with my wagon full of pipe-organ parts. David was absolutely fascinated by what I showed him. He ran his fingers over the brass and I could tell right then I had run across a stroke of pure luck. He handled the pieces like they were precious stones and if it hadn't been for his skills and incredible patience; I don't think that amazing conglomeration of pieces would have ever played music. David just thought of it like a giant watch; another puzzle of interconnected pieces that would run perfectly smooth if put together correctly.

David and a few of his kids followed me around like puppies until I finally gave in and made him a partner. I didn't pay him anything at first. I had about twenty dollars to my name when I first arrived and that was going fast. Of course twenty dollars at that time could rent you a room for six months with meals.

Someone said there might be a job open for a piano player, besides there was no shortage of weddings, birthdays and funerals. I wasn't too worried. Life was a lot slower back then and people were a lot more trusting. Money was something very few of us had. Our word and trade for labor was actually more valuable.

David didn't seem to mind the lack of funds; in fact, he kept saying things like, "we'll worry about money later. Let's get to work!"

When I secured the building and the bank account to go with it he was ecstatic. In fact, he was the one who took over the bookkeeping. I am a financial nightmare and if it hadn't been for David's skills at accounting, I probably would have gambled the whole project away the first year. As it was, we made a profit within just a few months and stayed in the black for as long as I lived.

David took over the place when I was killed and ran it until he died at the ripe old age of 59.

A heart attack took him one night when he was sitting at the organ. He was quietly playing one of his favorite Hebrew traditional songs when a jolt hit him. He went face-down on the keyboard. Nobody would have noticed until morning if he hadn't hit the volume pedal at the same time. A giant unknown chord blasted the townspeople awake and that was how he was found.

The funeral was a site to behold. His 13 children, and all their kids and most of the town showed up to see David off. He and I watched from the other side and thought "if they only knew." I was tempted to show up as a "stranger in town" to play the organ but one of his daughters took over the job and played so well I couldn't help sitting back and enjoying the show.

At first David had a hard time believing he was dead. You should have seen the look on his face when he saw me! I reassured him that all was well and God would be having a little talk with him soon and that on this side things were different but if he stayed in the right frame of mind, he could observe and help his family whenever he wanted. They just wouldn't know it was him.

Death always takes some getting used to but David was a very spiritual man and snapped out of it pretty fast. He worried a lot at first and hated to see the sorrow his death had caused but as he watched his wife and family take over the business, he knew all would be right in time. In fact, she ran things for over twenty more years. The family sold the building after her death for quite a profit and most of the original family soon moved out of Parker. His sons were responsible for developing the land around Aspen and have lived pretty well to this day.

At present, they own major holdings in real estate all over the mountain area and one of his grandsons is now developing the ski resort over the ridge from here.

I haven't seen David and Marlene for some time but once in a while they come back and we laugh about old times and drink to the future. He loves the idea that the old organ is still being used and even likes to pick up a "body" and go play it now and again.

Chapter Eighteen
Who Needs a Reason to Party?

Petunia was having so much fun setting up yearly celebrations and such that she decided to have one every other week throughout the summer season. The town would benefit from the extra tourist trade and the chances of meeting "Mr. Right" might just increase. I wasn't quite sure what she meant by Mr. Right, but I was willing to *be* him at any given notice if it wasn't for that pesky, I'm dead and she's not thing.

Petunia put together a committee of the local busybodies and came up with the "Festival For No Reason At All." They figured any festival was just an excuse to party and sell crafts and stuff anyway, so who needed a reason?

The non-profit committee got free advertising on television and radio as far away as Denver and Salt Lake City by offering to raise money for computers and art supplies for the kids at the MT Building.

The word got out and somebody at CNN picked up the story. Of course, by this time there were all kinds of rumors floating around as to the "real" reason for the festival and no one tried to deny any of them. In fact, they encouraged as many bogus reasons as possible. Someone was secretly sending out phony press releases (I plead the fifth). This was starting to snowball and so much misinformation hit the news that people were starting to arrive in droves weeks before the first festival was ready to kick off just to be the first to know what was really going on.

In the beginning, the townspeople thought it was real nice that they were getting notoriety and the businesses were having a record year. Just as suddenly, they realized how hard it is to park 2000 cars in a one-horse town. The mayor of Crawford, the town down the mountain, came up with the idea that there was plenty of parking in the Crawford meadows and the train could bring up the crowds, at a nominal fee of course. A split with Parker Town was arranged and the train was polished a little spiffier than usual. The schedule was tripled and a few older cars were taken out of mothballs. Before that time the train had been coming and going on Saturday and Sunday in the morning and the evening. It could handle around 300 people if they put on all the cars. This was fine until the rumor got out that Paul McCartney was going to jam with Lady Gaga and Madonna was going to come here just to 'kick her ass,' followed by a reunion of the entire cast of Saturday Night Live for the last 30 years. None of which was true. Okay, I never said I was perfect. I love a good white lie. It's the scoundrel in me.

One of the tabloids ran the rumor and before anyone could stop it, the town had grown from around 1500 to 50,000 people in a matter of three days.

Petunia didn't quite know what to think. One part of her thought of it like another Woodstock and the other part thought it was a nightmare. She was constantly approached by locals expressing both opinions vehemently to the point where she almost went into hiding which wasn't too hard in such a crowd.

The MT Building ran out of just about everything the first night. So did the cafe, the bakery, gas station and the market. We don't even want to talk about bathroom facilities!

Major and minor damage happened all over town with no one claiming responsibility. People camping in the woods burned down a few acres before the fire department could get through the crowd. They finally got it out before anyone was hurt. The train broke down and wouldn't be able to get parts for two weeks leaving several thousand mad people stranded 25 miles up the mountain and few thousand trying to find a place to stay in Crawford. Crawford put all they had up for sale and ran out of everything within a day or two. In Parker supplies were non-existent and trash was piling high. Several towns on the mountain brought in supplies that were suddenly worth triple. A bag of chips and a beer went for fifty bucks. People were setting up food sales in the back of pickup trucks and trailers announcing their location on Twitter. The town got on CNN all right, as the sight of a modern day disaster.

Two resourceful locals went into Denver and filled up a large U-Haul truck full of beer and sold it at three times the price. They almost ran that poor truck ragged going up and down the mountain. They rented an old army helicopter for the rest of the runs and made a small fortune. They pulled in enough money to cover tuition to a university. They are now both lawyers, but that's another story.

By the time the month was over Petunia was exhausted. She swore she'd never do it again. It took over two weeks just to pick all the trash out of the trees.

The MT Building made enough money to start a foundation for gifted kids and bought all new computers.

Personally, I had a great time at the festival. It was a whole lot easier on me than anyone else accept for the afternoon I spent as the fat guy who ate everything in sight. Ooh the pain! Why does Festival food have to taste soooo...good?

Chapter Nineteen

A Songbird Escapes the Vultures

In the chaos of the whole thing, over 50 people decided to make Parker Town their new home. One of them was a songwriter that would eventually put Parker Town on the map in a much better light.

Nashville was getting a little too crowded for a girl and her guitar. She had pounded the pavements, had her fill of broken dreams, broken appointments and just being broke all the time. She felt betrayed by several agents who always seemed to be looking down the front of her shirt or up her skirt more than at her writing.

"If I hear: '*Honey, you're the best there is. I'm going to make you a star,*' one more time! I'm going to be on trial for murder, torture and a whole lot of stuff I think about late at night! All I want to do is sing the songs I write, listen to the applause, and hopefully take home enough money so I don't have to have some crummy job to survive! Is that too much to ask?" she cried.

Her name was Julie. She had a last name but she thought it was prudent not to use it (I probably would have recommended dropping Gorphansnortch too). So she went by just plain Julie. If Cher and Adel could make a single name cool, so could she.

She really was an outstanding songwriter and played five instruments as well as anyone in Nashville. Not only that; she was pretty, had a cute figure and could dance as well as Miley Cyrus. Her four octave voice range was like a bird and she wasn't on any drugs. At 23, she was prime for stardom. She was also very spiritual and just couldn't bring herself to stoop to the level she had heard it would take to open the doors.

Depressed and almost broke she left the lights of Nashville without telling her boyfriend, who she was really beginning to dislike. Julie polished the dust off her credit card, wiped off the tears and drove her dad's mini-motor home as far west as Parker Town.

The first morning in Parker she felt like she had found paradise. This happens a lot in Parker. People either love it, or think of it as *a nice place to visit but who could live here*?

Julie met Petunia thinking she might get a job as a waitress; a career she had taken up more than once. At least with her smile and sweet spirit the tips were usually pretty good and besides it gave her cash in hand every day.

When Petunia saw the trailer Julie was pulling filled with instruments and sound equipment she promptly invited Julie to play for the kids.

Julie set up her little solo act kind of half-hearted as about 75 kindergarten through third grade kids came filing in. They all sat in neat rows in front of her and stared not saying a word. This was starting to unnerve Julie a little bit but she had played for worse and would get through it somehow, after all she thought, "I am a professional."

She set up a keyboard, a guitar, a microphone and a couple of speakers; just the minimum to get her through.

"How can they be so quiet?" she thought to herself. A little first-grader in the second row couldn't contain himself any longer. "Are you a musician?" he asked.

She started to make a smart remark like she was used to in the Nashville clubs and suddenly realized that this little innocent face was serious.

"Uh... yeah," she stammered as she looked away, trying desperately to think of what she was going to play. She had never performed for this age-group in her life and it terrified her. In high school she made extra money playing the piano in church, not babysitting.

I was sitting in *invisible mode* just off to her right, getting a kick out of her when I thought, *I'll bet she had a parent who sang songs for her when she was a child. If she started with that she would feel more at home.* I sent that thought to her like any good guardian angel and she picked it up like a winning lottery ticket.

The teacher left to go to the restroom and suddenly, as if on cue, all the kids started asking questions at once. Julie was astounded. *So that's why they were so quiet*!

She smiled and tried to answer as many questions as possible.

As she started to sing she realized her place in the whole scheme of things. The kids were the best audience she had ever played for. She extended the performance an extra hour and walked into Petunia's office three feet off the ground.

"Girl, you glow as if you just found out you are pregnant!" laughed Petunia.

"I think I am!" she laughed as she broke into tears of joy. "I think I just found my heaven."

"Well, welcome aboard. We've been looking for someone like you. The job pays lousy but we'll feed you, give you a place to park your motor-home and promise not to look down your shirt. The kids love you. The teachers said they can't stop talking about you. I know I was impressed. We're building a recording studio. Maybe you can help design it. Have you seen the pipe-organ yet?" laughed Petunia as she gave a Julie a tearful hug.

I slipped into the body of an older gentleman and was found playing the organ as Julie walked in. I just happened to know the songs she had learned as a child and brought her to tears as she sang along. We meet once a week now. She calls me Gramps and I call her Punkin'.

Julie's career in children's music has really started to take off. It turns out she has also found a talent for writing and illustrating kid's books. As her agent I am going to have a lot more influence on those fat-cats in Nashville and this time for all the right reasons.

After all, who can say *no* to an angel?

Chapter Twenty
Next Time I'm Leaving
The Bullets Home

One of the stranger things that ever occurred in Parker Town happened a few months ago. A retired couple in their late sixties was visiting our town. They both liked to drink and both like to get into fights... with each other. The fighting got so loud it woke *me* up on the *Other Side*.

I got out my handheld future reader and it said not to interfere. I was getting a little nervous as the woman staggered out to the car and retrieved a gun from the glove box. Then she walked back in and proceeded to plug him twice in the stomach. The bullets went right through his side without hitting anything major. He's lucky it was a .22 caliber. Also lucky he had only put two bullets in the gun.

The hotel manager called the sheriff, who called an ambulance. The man went to the hospital and she went to jail. Even though the bullets weren't fatal, it caused him a lot of pain and left a few scars. This incident also forced him to go into hiding while he recovered. He thought all along that she was capable of extreme hostility but up until now he didn't know how far it could go.

His wife, in the meantime, got bailed out of jail by some friend of hers and continued to stay as drunk and hostile as ever. She tracked down her husband and called him on the phone. It seems he was also her attorney and she wanted him to represent her in the upcoming attempted murder case. Is that a lot of nerve?

This is why I called it strange. For some unknown reason he loved and felt sorry for this woman who made his life miserable and treated him badly every chance she got; even as she dragged him into court. He was a damned good lawyer and put on an Oscar winning performance that got her off with six months probation, a month of community service and small fine.

Last I heard she was mad that she had to do a month of community service and tried to kill him again. He must like abuse because he told the judge that she was "off her medicine and didn't know what she was doing." Medicine? You call a quart of "Old Crow" medicine?

Life is just too weird at times. I also heard that the husband charged his wife $20,000 to represent her. It seems, she has her own trust fund her father, a rich but dying alcoholic, set up for her before she became an alcoholic. A pile of money she never shared with her husband.

Then the lawyer sued the doctor for malpractice because the gunshot wounds didn't heal as "soon as he thought they should." Another $50,000. It never ceases to amaze me how money can gravitate to such unworthy hands.

I have no idea how this is going to end but last I heard he keeps the bullets under lock and key and hides the kitchen knives before going to bed. He's driving a bright red new Mercedes convertible that he won't let her near. On the other hand, his twenty-year-old girlfriend has already wrecked it three times and wants him to buy her another one. He probably will, at a price.

Some people are beyond my help. In fact, I was talking to this couples' guardian angel the other day. She told me sadly that God has taken her off duty and is going to just let the chips fall where they may. All she has to do is see that nobody else gets hurt in the process. I'll bet they're in for a good talking to when they get to *this* side. From the looks of things that may not be too long. What usually happens is they get to be the guardian of someone just like them, the old mirror image.

Who says God doesn't have a sense of humor?

Chapter Twenty-one
God is in Charge of the Big Stuff
Angels Handle the Rest

It crossed my mind the other day that whoever reads this journal might be interested in what I do as a Guardian Angel. Sometimes I wonder myself. I do stay busy.

Most of my duties are both fun and heartwarming at the same time. Not to mention tragic, nerve-wracking, frustrating and mentally deranging. After all, we are dealing with human beings. Do I have to say more? You might call it a job. I call it a lifestyle. One I would highly recommend. I have news for you guys. You're all going to get a chance.

Here is an example of a typical day in the life of an angel. I was out walking the streets of Parker in invisible mode when an elderly lady started to trip over a pothole in the sidewalk. I checked my pocket-size Handheld Alternate Future Predictor (HAFP). The screen told me that if she tripped at that moment, her life would be miserable from then on. Broken hip, lots of pain, depression and a premature death. I hit the button that said whether or not it was all right to intervene and it flashed green for "go ahead." I reached for her foot with a gentle touch and lifted it a quarter of an inch higher. She never noticed and went along her way as if nothing had happened.

Personally, I like doing these little favors. It's fun and makes me feel needed. My Guardian Angel (yes, we have one too!) just lifted my finger as I almost hit the delete button on my lap-top. I would have had to start this journal all over. It's nice to know someone is there to catch you if you fall. Or, before you fall, as the case may be.

I am also the one who gets to greet people from Parker Town as they pass over to the Other Side and if I'm invited, I join them to watch their own funerals.

People are people and death doesn't change their personalities. Some folks are really surprised to see me and others are hostile. I don't make the decision where they go from here. I'm just the greeter and soother on Light Tunnel duty. My friend Molly sends them to their new homes.

Oh by the way, I forgot to tell you about Molly. She is such a sweetheart. She was raised in Parker Town and was about the same age as me before I died. A few months before my death, she was killed by a horse that thought he saw a rattlesnake. She was *my* greeter and is now my Guardian. We have been friends on this side ever since, nothing romantic, just friends. We help each other out and share a love for this little mountain town. I see her quite often and feel about as close to her as I have about anyone.

Romantic love is kind of an odd thing. It can make you crazy or it can make you secure. It can stand like a rock or change with the wind. So far it has been elusive and seems to hide when it sees me coming. I just try to have an open mind and wait patiently for the right one to come along.

Lately, I have had Petunia on my mind more than I think is comfortable. She is so independent. I love to see the way she handles the people at the MT Building. I just wish she wasn't such a mystery. I can't seem to break open the real Petunia. What I have seen, I really like, maybe even love. Of course, I'll have to wait until she comes over here and from the looks of things, barring some unforeseen accident, she will be alive and well in Parker for quite awhile. I'll have to be patient and just hope my heart doesn't do something weird, like, not move her foot when she's out rock-climbing and let her fall. These things even cross an angel's mind. We are not perfect you know.

On another note, I had the pleasure the other day to save a young couple from disaster. I love this job.

Marty Clemens just returned from college for the summer and thought it might be nice to spend a romantic day with Marjorie Thompson. He spent the previous day shining up his vintage 1967 Mustang fastback. More to impress himself than her. This was one of those muscle cars from the sixties that kept a lot of angels working overtime. Oh well, we like fast cars too, but hate to see the aftermath when they go over the cliffs around here. From this side death has a much happier perspective; we just hate to see the mess it makes. Yuck!

Marty packed a picnic lunch and tastefully arranged everything in a basket he had borrowed from his mother. Fried chicken, potato salad, well you know the routine. Even topped it off with a single red rose. What a guy!

So anyway, I checked in on my agenda for the day and found that I had to be up on Miracle Hill in time to keep this young couple from reaching the afterlife too soon or worse, finding themselves half-dead in the life-life. (Sorry I couldn't think of any other way to say it.)

Marty,19, was showing off. Marjorie, 18, was getting a little upset when they rounded Deadman's Curve at about 40 miles over the speed limit.

I had several choices to make at this point. Thank God for our time difference. I had plenty of time to choose. One second of Earth time can be stretched to an hour of angel time, or more if needed.

Warfare, bar fights and car wrecks really stretch the time continuum to the max. I checked my handheld reader where three choices were listed. Just a little bonus God threw into our angel lives that makes us feel as if we have a choice in the matter. It makes the job more fun and interesting. There is even a rewind if we don't like the results. Technology; ain't it great!

First choice: Let the car go over the cliff, crash and burn as the young couple who aren't wearing seatbelts fly out of the car windows, land in a tree and receive major cuts and bruises. Waste of a cool car.

Second choice: The car slows down. Nobody notices as I control the gas pedal. Uneventful. No lessons learned. Keeps the car safe.

Choice Three: She grabs the wheel. The car slides to a stop and they spend the day arguing. The car goes on to win vintage auto show awards for a fat bald guy who has plenty of money and no mechanical skills. The former owner, in this case Marty, has to sell the car to prove his love to get married. She spends the money on a mini-van that she will keep in the divorce the following year. Okay! It's not all perfection.

Oh yeah. Choice Four: They both get killed as I do absolutely nothing. Just kidding!

I chose a combination: I control the brakes and she grabs the wheel. They spend the day arguing and breakup. Turns out they were wrong for each other and this little incident was needed to make it clear to both of them. They each found the direction they were supposed to go and lived happily ever after. And if you believe that! I have some swamp land we are turning into timeshares I'd like to show you. At least we cleared up any notions they had toward each other at the time. The rest of the story isn't too important right now. Rest assured, some other Guardian had to work overtime with Marty when he moved to LA.

So anyway, these are a few of the duties I have as a Guardian Angel. I get new ones all the time and even travel to other worlds to help other angels from time to time. There doesn't seem to be any shortage of work. As an angel I have a good attitude toward my job and look forward to even the littlest of deeds because they can turn into (or avoid) such major outcomes. When something really spectacular comes up I'll let you know. Most of what I do would be considered mundane but I'll tell you when the person lands on this side, and gets to view the things we have done for them and what could have happened, that's when it's all worth it. We get big-time applause! Or ..."where the hell were you!"

Chapter Twenty-two

If There Isn't a Hell, This Family is Going to Create One

Even though I only lived in Parker Town as a human for a few years, my experience in this little piece of Heaven was one of the best times of my earth-life. I didn't have any financial worries and the people I met were, in general, pretty nice. But, once in a while one encounters the kind of human disaster that just doesn't seem understandable no matter how hard you try.

My Wings Got Lost with the Luggage

In the 1880s the Claiborne family was one of those anomalies that will leave you shaking your head and sometimes your fists. One minute they could be the worst gutter trash Hell could produce and the next minute they put angels to shame. It was like balancing on a knife edge. You never knew which side was going to appear and for how long.

There were eight daughters and seven sons, two dogs, a goat, and a poor old cat. The entire menagerie would usually roll into town all piled on a wagon that should have been thrown out a couple hundred years ago pulled by a pair of old oxen that were half deaf and the other half blind. A sort of pre-cursor to the mini-van.

You could hear the family arguing with each other for miles. The oldest daughter had a voice that could make brick crumble at a hundred yards and an attitude that made the meanest trappers and cowboys in Parker take the high side of the street. And she was the nicest of the bunch.

Here's the funny thing. Every one of those kids was extremely good looking. Six of the boys were over 6 foot four with curly thick hair and chins like Greek gods. The girls were tall too with wavy dark hair, big eyes and great figures from working outdoors. They ranged from 16 to 39 all living in a huge house they built out of local timber. The parents were in their early sixties but looked ten years younger. It must have been that good clean mountain air.

The Claibornes started a logging operation over the hill to the north and ran it with mostly family labor. They hired and fired the majority of Parker Town's able-bodied men within the first two years. Some were too scared to go back for their last paycheck.

The girls could handle the saws as well as the men and stood their ground in a squabble too. Fact is, they started most of the fights because they could out-work all of the local men and weren't shy about letting them know it. Nobody in the family dated much. Most of the boys around here were scared of either the Claiborne girls themselves or the father or the brothers. Not a lot of romance going on around that house. It left a lot of frustration and caused a lot of bruises but in general no one got seriously injured. A black eye here, a broken jaw there, at least nobody ever got shot.

My Wings Got Lost with the Luggage

The story that comes to mind centers around Little Josh. He was the youngest boy and by far the meanest. Josh was born premature so you see he didn't quite get all the looks that the others did or the height. The gene-pool must have been near empty by the time it got to him. His brothers and sisters towered over him. He was five foot, five inches. He developed a bad case of short complex. Of course, we just thought he was downright mean. We didn't need a fancy name for it. So he was picked on as much as possible and as the years went by he just got meaner and nastier to the point where not even his own family could stand him. It never occurred to them that they might be the cause of all this rage.

When he was around 14, he was run out of several of the neighboring towns and told not to come back. He used to stroll into the nearest saloon, step right up to the tallest man in the place and beat the holy crap out of him; then take on all comers. He'd come back to Parker with his knuckles all bloody, lot of scabs on his face, with this kind of weird look in his eye. He tried it with a couple of Gypsies camped by the river one afternoon. They knocked him cold and spent the day tattooing all kinds of evil things all over his chest and arms. By the time he came to, they were long gone and he felt like a pincushion. I have never seen a human being so mad in my life. Everyone in town got a great laugh out of that one, just not anywhere where he could hear it.

He was so humiliated that he ran off and joined the army. They threw him out after a couple of months. He beat up the toughest officer in the platoon and would have been thrown in the stockade if the fight hadn't been the Major's idea in the first place.

The fight was held outside of the fort and a whole lot of money changed hands. They had a rematch that was supposed to be fixed so the officer could save face. Josh couldn't stand to lose so he beat him severely again and made $500 on the deal.

A lot of enlisted men thought he was quite a hero until he whacked a few of them just for fun. The officers, enlisted men, and the Army head office came to a mutual agreement that Josh Claiborne was just too tough for this man's army. He had to leave in a hurry among a flurry of badly aimed bullets.

My Wings Got Lost with the Luggage

As you can imagine, nobody was glad to see Josh ride back into Parker. He didn't have any friends and even his family was getting scared of him. All but one.

I was sitting in the saloon one afternoon taking a nice day off with a cold glass of beer when Josh stumbles in. I was in an unusually good mood so I decided to be brave and order another glass and one for him too. Well it seems he was in a drinking mood and just happened to have a twenty dollar gold piece that he wanted to spend and since I had bought a round, he bought one, and then I bought one, and the next thing you know we were long lost buddies, arm in arm, tears streaming down our faces, crying in our beer over how *the world has been treating us rotten and for absolutely no good reason that we could see*. So right about this time the door opens and I see Josh look up and say under his breath, "Oh shit!"

"Joshua Claiborne! You stand up and give a lady respect!" demanded a little tiny gray-haired lady a few ounces short of a hundred pounds fully dressed, as she literally grabbed him by the ear and dragged him into the street. I stood up, a little wobbly, fully expecting to get hauled out too.

"Who the *hell* was that?" I asked the bartender as we both looked on in amazement.

"I think that was Grandma Claiborne. If you value your life, I wouldn't make any comments within earshot, especially if you want this building to remain intact." laughed the bartender nervously. Somehow I think he was serious. I'm not sure which of the two he was more nervous about. My money was on Grandma.

We watched as she spent the next five minutes raking Josh up one side and down the other. Swinging her arms and quoting scriptures. He looked like a pit bull that had just been hit hard between the eyes with a two by four. His chin was stuck to his chest and his feet were pigeon towed in. His shoulders all slumped. If he'd had a tail it would have been dragging on the ground.

The bartender and I were trying to think of ways to escape when Josh put his arm around Grandma and tried to kiss her on the cheek. She wouldn't have anything to do with it. She let go a right uppercut that would have made Mohammed Ali proud. The last we saw of Josh he was following that little old lady about ten feet behind begging on a stack a Bibles for forgiveness.

That night he came back to the saloon and met his match. A young lady he tried to force out of the bar pulled a derringer and shot him twice in the head. The local sheriff just told her to leave town. Nobody would follow, not even the family.

I met Josh on this side. He still has an attitude and likes to go back to Earth now and then as a bad example. You might have even seen him. Last trip to Earth he was the head of a political party in Germany in the 1930s. He kept a whole lot of angels working double-shifts.

Some people take an eternity to learn and others are put here for us to enjoy the commotion they create. Josh knows how to fill the bill.

Chapter Twenty-three
A Family Made From Spare Parts

In a town as small as Parker Town in the 1800s each and every person's skills can be of great importance and regard, especially if he or she is the only one for miles.

This story is about a man whose skills became famous because he went out of his way to be extremely good at what he did and shared the results of his labor. His name was Eli. He was a shoemaker who came to Parker as a child with a family from Italy.

Eli was discovered hot, sweaty and thirsty in Atlanta, Georgia, under a wooden doorstep by Mrs. Milano when he was around 4 years old.

She fed him, fell in love with his big brown eyes, his sweet smile and praised God for delivering him to her. The note pinned to his dirty shirt said: *Please give him a loving home. His parents are dead.   He's a good boy.*

Mrs. Milano had no intentions of giving him back when her husband suggested they find his family and after a few days you would have had to pry Eli away from both of the Milano's with a small army.

She talked her husband into leaving the south for a new life out west just to get him to a place where he could be free. They both felt that slavery was an abomination in the sight of God. They risked their own lives as they smuggled this little Negro boy into a home built wagon and headed for the Rockies. She and her husband had no children of their own because of a horse injury when her husband was a teen, but not out of choice. Along the journey they picked up three more "strays" and built a family out of "spare parts."

Both she and her husband were very intelligent and hardworking. A skilled craftsman, Anthony Milano came from several generations of shoe and boot makers who were famous in Europe for creating not only style and quality but a wonderful fit.

Olga Milano was an orphan Russian immigrant in her teens that had found her way to Italy where she learned the Italian language and fell in love with Anthony. They were married just a few months later and decided to seek their fortune in the United States. When they came to America they both had to learn English to survive.

Mrs. Milano's skills were in the sales and accounting departments. She loved people and also kept the books to the penny. They fell in love with Parker Town the minute they saw it and decided this was where they were going to set up shop.

There was a storefront for sale on the main street. The owner was willing to accept a small down payment and take the rest on a percentage of the business. It was the best move the owner ever made and his feet thanked him too. One good thing about being the only shoemaker for a hundred miles is, "when you are needed, you are *really* needed." Their reputation grew and so did their skills.

Of course both the Milano's could cook incredible Italian food so they subsidized their income by making dinner available every night in the front of the shoe-shop during the summer. The couple grew garlic and basil, created homemade pasta and baked the best tasting bread on the mountain. People were always trying to steal the recipes. The biggest problem was acquiring good olive oil and Italian cheeses in such an out-of-the-way place.

The Milano's learned to substitute a lot of different things but very few of the customers complained. The food was better than anything anyone had ever tasted and soon they had to buy the building next door just to handle the traffic.   That building still houses the original restaurant that is still open today serving Olga's recipes proudly to a sold out crowd every night.

Eli started working around the shop when he was around five or six. He loved the smell of leather and found the place to be friendly and warm. He liked to work hard and tried to imitate anything he could by following his adopted father everywhere he went.

Eli's voracious appetite followed his mother around in the evenings where he learned to cook and wait on tables. She used to tease him about eating up all the profits. Everybody loved Eli who always had a big smile on his face.

Eli got along with everyone. His adopted Father, Anthony Milano, used to stand back and look at this oversize, big-eyed, happy-faced kid and tears would come to his eyes. "How could anyone just leave him?" he thought. He loved that boy more than anything and Eli knew for sure he had a permanent home.

Eli's birth parents must have been big people because he grew into just about the largest man in Parker. When he was 17, he was six foot 4 and 265 pounds with chubby cheeks and a warm smile but not an ounce of fat. He was strong from hard work and had a gentle personality.

Eli was a welcome sight at the annual 4th of July, Parker Town picnic tug-of-war contest. Each team would give him friendly bribes for weeks ahead to get him to choose their side. The team offering the best food usually won his services. Eli wasn't allowed in the pie-eating contest for obvious reasons but he always had more than he needed anyway because his mom made the pies.

As a child, Eli was large enough that the kids in school didn't tease him about the color of his skin. Not to his face anyway. In a town as small as Parker at the time, less than 300 people, you either got along or you didn't. It was quite a melting pot in those days and most people took you for face value.

He was a gentle giant and since most of the kids grew up with him he just became another kid. He had several friends that he considered close. They stayed friends until they passed over to this side. In fact, they are still good friends over here.

Eli was as black as an African-American can get, almost blue. His mother used to kid him when she came into kiss him goodnight. "Open your mouth so I can see you!" she would laugh and so would he. They loved each other dearly and spent hours together. She taught all the kids to read and speak Italian and Russian. Anthony taught the kids Italian and French.

The Milano family got a kick out of carrying on conversations with the various immigrants who drifted through town who were shocked to hear this big Negro kid speaking fluently in their language. Eli was always happy to learn something new and read everything he could get his hands on.

His quality of education and eloquent speech saved him from the local prejudices. In a town the size of Parker there is a lot of interdependence and it doesn't pay to make enemies. The townspeople learned to overlook their own biases passed on by their parents and made the family feel right at home for as long as they lived.

Of course, crossing Mrs. Milano was considered extremely dangerous. She had a loud passionate Russian/Italian temper that proved to be more bark than bite but nobody wanted to test her patience too far and that included Eli.

Everything was going along on a pretty even keel. The boot business had been getting better as word got out that the quality was worth the price.

The problem was Eli. At 13, he had already reached puberty and the hormones were racing. He was having trouble concentrating. For the first time in his life, he was starting to feel like he was different. He started to get withdrawn. It was the first time that he had ever felt lonesome.

His parents knew this day would arrive but just left it in the back of their minds. Now it was hard to ignore.

They knew this was going to happen with all their kids, after all, they had picked up children from the back alley that were of several mixed races. The twin girls were some kind of Indian-Mexican mix and the other boy was Chinese. If you think the black kid got looks speaking Italian, you should have seen the double-takes when the Chinese kid answered him in French as the twins argued in Russian, Spanish and Navaho.

Eli was the same age as the twins and a year older than his brother. They fought and made up just like any other siblings. Bonded together like a rock if someone outside the family tried to give anyone a hard time. They were, when you got down to basics really not much different than any typical family of the day. They just had a lot more skills.

Eli used to like to go with his father down to Texas to pick up leather for the shoe factory. This time something happened that would change his life.

Eli and Anthony took the train to Amarillo. They rented a large wagon to go out to one of the ranches that had their own tannery. Leather was cheaper if you could buy it from the source. Anthony liked to hand pick the skins for consistency. On their way they passed a large house with a sign that said: *St. Mary's Catholic Orphanage.*

"What's that?" asked Eli.

"It's a home for children who have no parents," replied Anthony. "They live there until someone comes to adopt them."

Eli sat silent for moment. He had been told how he was found and adopted but it made him sad to think of others not as lucky as he.

"Do you think there might be room in our house for a new baby?" asked Eli. "I'd like to have a little brother or sister."

"Let's go see." said Anthony who was a sucker for kids.

They went up to the door and knocked. An elderly nun came to the door and asked what they wanted.

"We want a baby!" laughed Eli.

The nun got such a kick out of Eli's obvious innocence that she just laughed and invited them in.

"Come in out of the sun and tell me what this is all about," said Sister Sarah as she motioned for the pair to sit down. She was doing everything she could to keep from laughing. *Dignity of the office and all that.* Her bright blue eyes gave her away.

Eli was distracted by a girl who was sweeping the hall. She turned away shyly as he stared. She was as black as he was. The first Negro he had ever seen other than the one in the mirror. She was absolutely beautiful. His mouth hung open and his eyes glazed over. The next words he spoke came out like he had a mouth full of mud. He was stopped dead in his tracks.

She was dumbfounded too. They just stood there staring for a good 10 seconds before coming to consciousness again. She realized it before he did and ducked around the corner. She stood there with her heart racing as she got up enough nerve to come up with an excuse to see Sister Sarah.

In the meantime, Anthony was telling the Sister about their makeshift family and how his wife had talked about maybe adopting a couple more, hopefully babies this time. He had good credentials and earned enough to keep a family that size comfortable. Sister Sarah could see he was sincere as he wiped the tears from his eyes when he spoke about his family. Adoption back then was much easier if you had good references.

"Bring your wife here as soon as you can so we can fill out the necessary legal forms. We have to do a background check but if you bring a judge's letter from the city where you live it's all you need and will speed up the process."

"Thank you so much Sister! We will be back in two weeks," laughed Anthony who was so excited he could hardly stand it. "Eli! Let's go get the leather and bring your mother the good news! ELI! Let's go!" he shouted.

Eli couldn't think of anything outside of that pretty chocolate colored girl. He was unusually quiet and had a dreamy look in his eye all the rest of the trip.

"I think our boy is in love," said Anthony to his wife when they got home.

The whole family went back two weeks later and met with Father McKinley. He was a fat jovial man who loved kids and was very happy when one of his was placed in a good home. They spoke in French and Italian; a real treat for the Father who had been schooled in Paris and Rome.

My Wings Got Lost with the Luggage

The Milano's retold the story of Eli and the rest of their family. Father McKinley was very impressed. Anthony promised a pair of shoes for each of the 30 kids in the orphanage and a small donation of cash for the church. The Milano's were approved and very happy. Now came the time to choose.

As they were entering the hallway the pretty black girl who had caught Eli's heart came around the corner and stood shyly as they passed. She followed the Milano's as they looked over the three babies that had arrived in the last few weeks.

Mrs. Milano took the Father aside and asked about the girl.

"Her name is Mary. She's 15 years old and her parents were killed in a snowstorm. She was working as a dishwasher in a soup kitchen when she was raped by the owner one night after work. She came into our parish cold and terrified. She has been here for just a couple of months but she is still very scared. She is the sweetest girl you would ever want to meet. Turns out she is pregnant and will have the baby here. We can keep her here until she is 16 but I don't know what is going to happen after that. She might have to give the baby up for adoption and find a new place to live. Would you like to meet her?" asked Father McKinley.

"I know my son hasn't stopped talking about her. If we were to adopt her then would she be his sister? And if they fell in love they couldn't get married? But what if we just took custody? Would they be free to let nature take its course? What do you think Father?" asked Mrs. Milano.

"Yes, I suppose you have a point there. Would you be willing to take care of her child too?" asked the Father McKinley.

"Of course! The more the merrier!" laughed Mrs. Milano.

That is how fate brought a family together creating one of the strongest bonds Parker Town has ever seen.

Eli and Mary were feeling the pains of love. As they slowly got to know each other. They would build a rock-solid bond of friendship long before romance took over.

Eli was a little younger than Mary and within six months she had a little girl. She was still mourning the loss of her parents. The rape was still fresh in her mind too. The Milano's did everything they could to make her feel loved. Their hearts just about burst when the baby was born.

Eli's parents had long talks with him and didn't hold anything back about marriage, love and the responsibility it requires. Eli just sat with a silly grin and took it all in. Mary was all he could think about.

At first, Eli had to settle for being in love at a distance but he knew she was the one and only. She knew it too, but still liked to play hard to get. She could get Eli to do anything for her. The baby's arrival sealed his fate. He was right there helping his mother with the birth. This experience created in Eli a whole new respect for women. He married her a year after the baby was born and never thought of it as anything but his own.

He became one of the county's leading citizens and one of the best shoe, boot and saddle makers in the state. By the time they both died in their nineties. They had 11 kids, 24 grandkids and 5 great-grandkids. Most of them still live in Parker Town.

Chapter Twenty-four

Kids and Dynamite
A Wonderful and
Creative Combination

Parker, like any other small town in the 1890s had quite a variety of personalities, attitudes, skill levels and intelligence levels; all in some kind of synchronicity that kept them from harming each other most of the time; a funny balance that changed day by day; some good, some not so good.

Weeks could go by where nothing worth mentioning occurred. If it wasn't for the fact that the townspeople loved telling stories about great events, I think more than a few of the folks would have gone crazy with boredom, especially in winter when the snow got over 5 feet high in the streets. Of course, every time it did there was an old codger who recalled a few years back when "the snow drifted over the rooftops." It's kind of like the *fish that got away story*. Every time it's told the fish gets bigger and the snow gets higher. He was also the one who had to walk 15 miles in the snow to school, barefoot, uphill both ways. *It was so cold it took half the day just to chip the dogs off the fire hydrants.*

In a little town like Parker Town there is always a story that gets passed down through the generations. Usually by the time you hear a version it isn't even close to the original event, but still, a good story is a good story. This one happened to Eli Milano.

When Eli was 12, he and a couple of his buddies were looking for adventure. They found a box full of dynamite in an old abandoned mine. They figured it might be fun to shinny up the flagpole in the center of town and tie a stick to the ball on top. Freddy, 10, was the smallest, so he volunteered to shinny up the pole. He fastened the dynamite at the top with some twine and dropped a length of detonating chord down to Eli who promptly put a match to it. They ran as fast as they could and just rounded the corner by the general store in time to hear the explosion. The concussion from the blast knocked out every window for almost a quarter of a mile. The boys gasped in amazement looking at each other like death warmed over.

"Oh my gosh! What the hell are we going to do now?" gulped Freddy who was turning white. Eli almost turned white too.

"Uh, uh, uh, I don't know! We better hide until we can figure out what to do." cried Eli.

The train was headed down the hill so without even thinking they hopped on board. Three boys have never looked so scared in all their short lives. First of all, they had never been on the train before. They were lucky to duck inside just as a big tree-branch almost knocked them off. The car they were in was the garbage car that hauled trash and refuse down the mountain once a week. It smelled awful but the boys were too scared to notice.

It was almost dark when they arrived at the train station in the little town of Crawford. They suddenly realized how poorly planned this whole thing was. They spent the night up a tree because Jimmy thought he saw a bear. They tried hard to get a little sleep.

In the morning they woke up baggy-eyed, stiff, cold and scared with the realization that the train only goes back up the mountain once a week. They just looked at each other and tried to hold back the tears.

"Well, now what?" the other boys shouted at Eli as if it was all his fault.

"How the heck am I supposed to know? What do I look like an information office?" he growled. He was just as scared but because of his size they looked up to him.

"First thing we gotta do is find something to eat. Sleeping in the top of a tree gets me pretty darned hungry. Any of you got any money?" asked Eli.

Nobody had any money. So they wandered near town to see what they could scrounge up. Almost every house in the 1800s had a backyard garden. This town was no exception. The boys got their first meal from the farmer's melon patch and figured a few peaches wouldn't be missed either.

By now, the Parker Town sheriff had been notified that three boys were missing and everyone was frantically looking for them. The blast on top of the flagpole was looked upon as the "crime of the century and whoever had done it probably kidnapped the kids too."

The parents and half the town gathered in the square to set up a search station. The other half was cleaning up broken glass. Telegrams were sent out on all the wires to keep a look out for a big Negro kid and a couple of towheads with freckles. They weren't considered dangerous but were probably cold and hungry.

Meanwhile the boys filled up their shirtsleeves with peaches and sat on a big rock by the lake trying desperately to come up with a plan.

"My Dad is gonna kill all of us!" cried Freddie as the peach fuzz started making him itch.

Jimmy just sat their quietly scratching and moaning. He kept saying, "This is bad. This is *really* bad!"

"Maybe we just ought'a start walking. It's only twenty-five miles. We could make it by nightfall," suggested Eli. "Maybe they won't have noticed we were gone."

"Oh sure. My mother must be going crazy by now. She's probably beatin' the hell out of both my little brothers just to get practiced up for what she's gonna do to me. I don't know about you guys. I'm scared!" blabbered Freddy between tears.

On the other side of the lake were several colorful wagons in a circle with a group of people dressed like nobody the boys had ever seen. Easily distracted as young boys are, their sense of adventure kicked in.

"Let's sneak up on them and see what's going on." said Eli as they crept through the high grass toward the camp.

Eli could hear the Gypsies talking in Italian and figured they might be able to trade peaches for a hot meal if he talked to them right. Just when they were getting up the nerve to go up to the camp Eli heard a scream and turned around to see a large Gypsy man who had Jimmy by the throat. "What the hell are you kids doing?" he screamed in Italian.

"We were just looking to make friends!" cried Eli not realizing he had shifted into Italian.

"You speak Italian! laughed the big Gypsy, "Come my friend, come and share a good breakfast."

The boys weren't all that hungry but who could turn down such hospitality? They shared the peaches and drew smiles from the ladies.

Everyone gathered around the big Negro kid who spoke their language like a native. They all hit him with questions at once. "What part of Italy are you from? What is your name? What are you doing here?"

He explained things as well as he could but when he got to the reason they were running away the Gypsies couldn't hardly stop laughing. Then a hush came over the clan as they realized they might get implicated in the crime. Kidnapping wasn't something they wanted to get involved in, unless it meant a lot more money than this young shoemaker was worth.

"I think it's time you children were on your way," said the leader. "Good luck. It was nice to hear our language spoken by someone other than us."

"Please come visit," said Eli. "My parents would love to hear the language too. They would love to hear stories of the old country."

They were given a sack filled with bread and cheese and sent back up the mountain. The boys were still nervous but knew it was the right thing to do. It was almost dark when three tired and dusty boys approached the town. Several people saw them and ran to tell the parents. Eli spent the next hour making up the most elaborate story a 12 year old could conger up. It included masked men, bears, hiding in trees, Gypsies and an incredible escape unharmed. An adventure that made most of the local kids jealous and placed the parents in a state of amazement. They were so enthralled by his story, they forgot about all the broken glass as they thanked God for the boys safe return.

Not for long. Jimmy couldn't stand the pressure and finally confessed. The three boys had to work off the debt for the next two years. The silver lining in this little tale was the fact that the younger boys learned to work with glass and started a business that thrived in Parker for many years raising two families with a total of 13 kids.

Eli discovered something in him that he had previously left untouched. Imagination. He had really been exhilarated by the story that poured out of his mouth like a tidlewave. Eli took up writing that night after his chores were done. He questioned every new stranger in town and learned everything he could about the outside world. His father read his stories and turned them in to the Crawford newspaper that always needed something to print.

His stories about a trapper nick-named Rocky Mountain became a monthly column. They were so well liked by the people of Parker that the stories caught the attention of a larger paper in Denver. The editor of the newspaper couldn't believe it was written by a twelve year old Negro boy.

At first they were not going to print it because of just that but after reading several weeks columns they knew that talent outweighed their prejudices. Eli was a hit. He was approached by a publisher and given a one-hundred dollar advance on a book; a small fortune in those days.

As he got older the series of books sold quite well. He traveled all over the world telling his stories and selling books but his heart was always home with his wife and kids in Parker Town.

"I still long for the smell of leather and love to work with my hands," he laughed proudly as he held up his latest creation, a new saddle for his granddaughter.

He wrote stories up to the age of 93 and still made his own shoes. The highlight of Eli's life was the day he met Mark Twain who had come to Parker just to meet him.

The little shoe shop is still in Parker, a historical landmark. Eli's Grandson owns it and keeps it just like it was when it was first started. It's quite a tourist attraction. The family has grown to over 40 members who all love to hear the stories Great-Grandpa Eli wrote. There are plans to do a documentary of his life.

Eli and I still like to visit the mountains around Parker. Sometimes we just sit on a rock in silence and enjoy the view. He hasn't run out of stories and I haven't run out of time to listen to them. Sometimes I like to share one of mine. He sits and smiles.

Chapter Twenty-five

You Can't Con a Con.

Can You?

I was thinking back to the 1890s and some of the characters that left an impression on me. One of them was ol' Jasper. When I first met him he was a robust little man about 70 years old. He had been stomping around the mountains near Parker for over 40 years and knew just about everyone within 200 miles.

When he first came to town not too many people took notice. He was accompanied by an old mule named "Fizzle" and a horse named "Pop." The names reflected the animal's personalities especially the funny way they passed gas, which was quite often and in large amounts. He had another horse named "Ma" that died on the trail into Parker. Before she died he liked to say it was a "Ma and Pop operation that fizzled" with a glint in his eye.

By the time I met Jasper he was old and bent, but from what I hear, he was quite a handful when he was younger. He had steel gray eyes that never missed a thing and hands that felt like shoe leather. Worst of all, Jasper had a cutting sense of humor that grated on you if you let it. Jasper got punched in the nose more than once by a drunken cowboy who didn't think he was kidding.

Jasper claimed to be a prospector but was really a hunter by trade and a gambler by choice.

He made the bulk of his money the first month in Parker Town by out-shooting just about everyone for five miles in every direction and winning bets. This made two kinds of impressions. He felt safe in the idea that people might think he was tougher than he really was and it gave him a bit of celebrity status. He didn't care about all the folks that would like to get their hard-earned currency returned but stayed out of the shadows at night just in case.

A set of whiskey bottles was placed high up on the fence post and crowds would gather. The local sheriff handled the bets. They would have really cleaned up if it weren't for a shortage of shooters who were willing to try their hand. They had to wait until summer brought in the tourists. Even at 70, I swear Jasper could still put a piece of lead up a squirrels butt at 100 yards. Of course there isn't much call for that sort of thing anymore.

This part of the story happened way before I met him. It was told to me by one of the local old-timers.

What made Jasper colorful was the way his whole countenance would change when he zeroed in on a new, poor unsuspecting out-of-towner. The dollar signs would flash in his eyes and I swear he stood 6 inches taller. He would grab the latest sucker by the arm and lead him into a world that was instantly filled with good life, overnight riches, and Shangri-La provided he joined up with Jasper and made a small investment in an *already successful* mining operation.

"Why if I was to go down just another five or six feet, there is enough silver down there to make the King of England look like a gutter rat!" he would say as he produced a pouch full of silver from his coat pocket and rolled it around in his palm. He had a pitch that would have made Al Capone proud.

He had roughly three months in the summer to talk an investor into a grubstake. For those of you who don't know what a grubstake is: it is everything a miner needs to get him through the winter without having to work or go into town; usually provided by a sucker who thinks there is going to be big money for everyone.

He would always talk a big line to a few greedy lowlanders that would pool their money. This would give him enough cash to keep a stake in a local poker game for the winter and still have enough left over for whiskey, a warm fire, sowbelly, grits and a couple of evenings with Geraldine, the Parker Town lady of the evening. He lived simply, but he stayed well fed and loved, for the right price.

Jasper slept in a one room shack down by the river a couple of miles from Parker with an amazing view. He loved the view and could sit out there for hours in his old rocker dreaming up new schemes for the summer.

The funny thing is, Jasper never shoveled a drop of ore out of that mountain. I don't know where he got the pouch. Come to think of it, it was always the same pouch. He owned the claims legally but I think he won them in a card game. Whoever owned the claim before probably thought Jasper got the worst of the deal. There were over 200 holes in the ground, none of which produced anything but dirt.

Two of Jasper's grandsons started snooping around after he died and struck it rich. Turns out he was right about one thing. There was ore down there but it turned out to be tungsten and not silver. They dug out enough to get rich, turn to alcohol and piss it all away on what they thought was unlimited recreation. I guess it runs in the family. The ore ran out and so did they.

I met both of them in Heaven. They said it was a lot of fun but they would have done it different if given another chance.

Getting back to Jasper; at 70 years old he played an old beat-up banjo and the fiddle along with a couple of the locals who played guitars, standup bass, piano, harmonica and a raggedy looking old snare drum.

On Saturday night they used to come in to the MT Building to "raise the roof a few notches." Sometimes I sat in on the organ but it didn't quite fit. I had about ten-times the volume and a tendency to drown out the other instruments. I could also play the piano and took turns with the other piano player.

At first, the group put up with my pipe-organ talents but after I got to know them better, they quit being polite and told me to "get the hell off the stage or else evil things were going to happen to my first born." I owned the place but had a soft-spot in my heart for musicians. I just watered down their whiskey and helped gamble away their paychecks like most of the saloon owners of the day. They always had a meal and a roof if they didn't drink too much. Or even if they did, most of the girls in the brothel thought of the musicians as pets and took good care of them no matter what condition they were found in. It was just a big weird sort-of family. We all had a great time. Actually, these are some of my best memories of the old MT.

I liked to play the piano and learned to accompany the ladies who thought they could sing. Then I'd end up dancing with them while the players turned green with envy. I'd throw a gold piece in the tip jar and make them play all the songs I knew they hated just to drive 'em nuts.

Getting back to Jasper...

Jasper had a beat-up old dog named Clutz that followed him everywhere he went. He was big and ugly and hadn't had a bath in his whole life except for the time the horse cut loose on him. I still think that horse did it on purpose. I guess you could say that was more of a shower than a bath. His fur was matted all over from rolling in the mud and his tail had a chunk out of it where a bear made a believer out of him. I don't even want to talk about his problem with skunks and porcupines.

Anyway, this old dog loved to hunt more than anything in the whole world. Jasper wouldn't have to say a word. All he had to do was pull the rifle down from the rack over the fireplace and that mutt would go crazy. He'd spin around howling, barking and rolling around on the floor. You'd think the dog had just hit the lottery. Jasper used to haul down the gun when friends came over just for a good laugh.

This is the story the way Jasper told it.

I was out in the woods with that stupid dog, hunting elk, when nature come a'calling. I was squatted down in the middle of the trail with my pants down around my ankles when I hear a big commotion up behind me. It must have been twenty yards to my rear. I looked up just in time to see this four point buck come flying over my head. Ripped my hat right off. I didn't have time to grab my gun or my pants when this damn dog come roaring through the bushes at a full charge, right up my butt. I tell you haven't lived 'till you been cold-nosed by 70 pounds of Labrador Retriever going 20 miles an hour. We both went flying. He just looked at me with crap all over his nose and one of those dumb-dog looks as if to say, 'boy that was fun! Now what'ya want to do?' He's darn lucky my rifle wasn't within reach or he'd a'been the trophy on my outhouse door that year.

My Wings Got Lost with the Luggage

Jasper was a dedicated bachelor until the day he met up with Beatrice McGee, or "Bee" as she liked to be called. He used to call her the "old hornet" behind her back.

Somehow they got to talking about what business he was in and he, mistakenly, used his get-rich spiel on her. She was greedy enough even though she had a ton of money in the bank from a long-dead husband and didn't mind losing a few bucks if there was a goodtime involved. She had lived on her own long enough to know a shyster when she saw one but she was also attracted to scoundrels and here is the rest of the story.

Bee turned over a pretty large grubstake to Jasper just before the fall snow. Jasper was living pretty high on the hog spending Bee's money as winter approached but hadn't counted on Bee staying in town to watch the progress in the mines. Usually by the first snowfall the lowlanders went home and left him to enjoy the calm of winter. Come summer Jasper would whip up a sob story as to how after laboring all winter *all the money had been used up with no big silver strike and would you please forgive me?* He was so good at this (tears and all) that most of them just felt sorrier for him then for themselves and ended up leaving town. *That poor man all that suffering up in the snow.*

Jasper made a policy of only taking small amounts from a lot of people rather than a large amount from one. People give up easier trying to get back a little loss than a big one.

Well, Bee was a little feistier than that. She bought the local hotel and livery stable and proceeded to dig in for the winter. This made Jasper nervous. When he gets nervous he likes to drag out a jug of that moonshine he's been stillin' up in the hills with a couple of his friends. He's not the best drinker in the world and sometimes his mouth gets ahead of his brain.

Word got back to Bee that Jasper was a con and she decided to see what she could do about straightening him out. The money didn't mean a thing to her. She was bored and loved the game. Beside she had a bit of a crush on ol' Jasper and liked to follow him around. She was one of the few who actually liked his sense of humor. Payback is tough. Her sense of humor drove him nuts.

My Wings Got Lost with the Luggage

One of Bee's friends, a fat, dark-haired lady, 35 years old and mother of five, was in on the deal and between them they conjured up a scheme to get back at Jasper.

It just so happens that a gentleman was staying at the hotel that looked just like everyone's stereotype of a modern lawyer. Since nobody had actually seen a lawyer in Parker Town. He fit the bill. He was really an encyclopedia salesman from Denver who liked to travel to get away from his nasty wife and three ugly step-kids. Anything to prolong going home was fine with him as long as there was money in it. He had a vested suit with a gold-chained pocket watch, a pair of Italian shoes and a briefcase made out of alligator from New Orleans. He was the perfect one to play the part. With his hair slicked down and vest buttoned up, he just reeked of success. He even practiced looking mean in the mirror. All he had to do was think of his marriage and the right face for the job magically appeared.

Bee had enough money to set him up in luxury for awhile. She even bought out all of his encyclopedias. Johnny McDougal was a happy camper except for the fact that he had to stay hidden until the right moment.

Bee supplied him with more booze and food than he could stand and filled in the rest of his time with the company of the local saloon girls. When it was over Johnny complained more about having to leave than having to stay. I think he had a bit of a crush on Bertha the Swedish girl. I know she had one on him that ended when he ran out of money and talked about going back to his wife.

The team rehearsed for several days and polished the act. *Jasper was going to get it this time.* They even paid-off the local judge, sheriff and a few others to make it look authentic and prevent any screw-ups.

Bee had a warrant for his arrest drawn up and had it served. The charges were rape and criminal assault on a lady. The victim being Bee, the charges were being pressed by the sheriff and not the lady herself. She did not want to press charges but the sheriff, after a few dollars entered his pocket, was claiming to have seen the perpetrator in the act and was held by the law to see it to court.

They hauled Jasper kicking and scratching off to jail where he spent the night crying, screaming and hollering about how innocent he was and if he ever got out of this jail he was "gonna see that somebody paid for this injustice." He even came up with a few new forms of profanity that I had never heard before.

By this time the whole town had heard about the dastardly deed and was already taking bets as to his guilt or innocence. The newspaper finally had something to write about and the saloon was humming. The Ladies Guild was getting ready to hang him up by his genitalia and the local preacher found more material than he could use in one hour so he extended the service to an hour and a half. Nobody slept through that sermon except ol' Bert who is deaf and likes to go to church to get away from his crabby wife.

It was time to bring the fake lawyer on the scene. He boarded the train about a mile out of town and showed up in all his glory due to a little "pre-arrival publicity." Of course that didn't take much. All Bee had to do was tell a few of the Bingo Club members, and half the town showed up at the platform.

Meanwhile, Bee went to visit Jasper in jail. She had a big bandage over one eye and one on her arm. It took a few minutes to calm him down and explain to him that she wasn't the one pressing charges. She had hired a lawyer for him and "would he please meet with him." She was even sounding sympathetic, "You don't really know what happens when you drink," she said in her most pathetic voice followed by a little sniffle and a tear created by an onion in her pocket.

By this time Jasper was getting scared that he might get hung for something he didn't remember doing and if a lawyer was what it took to get him off then "bring him on."

The fake lawyer went into his routine and explained the charges. The crime could merit a life sentence or two, hanging, torture, dismemberment and a hundred years of hammering rocks. Not to mention all kinds of cruel unspeakable things that could happen if the townspeople got to him first. The lawyer really used all his sales skill to absolutely terrify Jasper and when he had him crying and pleading for a loophole; the lawyer came up with a doozy.

"If you were married to Bee, then all the charges would have to be dropped, because you were just exercising your rights as a husband," said the lawyer as serious as he could be without laughing. He knew this was the clincher.

Jasper just went stone cold silent. Somehow he just couldn't picture himself married to anyone, let alone "The Hornet!"

"I'll give you an hour or two to think about it and if you decide, I can get a judge over in Cody to sign a marriage certificate and back date it to last month," he said as he signaled to be let out of the cell.

"What about Bee? Do you think she would go along with it?" Jasper asked hesitantly.

"Bye for now, I'll see you tomorrow," said the fake lawyer as he tried hard not to bust out laughing. "I need a drink," he thought to himself.

That night Jasper hardly slept. He even tried prayer for the first time in his life. "God, if I ever get out of this, I promise never to horns woggle anyone the rest of my days!" he cried with about as much sincerity as he had when he was taking someone else's money.

Bee came to visit and told Jasper that the lawyer had informed her of the situation. She seemed to think the whole thing was pretty funny. Now her sense of humor was really grating on him.

"I was attacked from behind. I guess we'll never know who really did this to me. He's probably long-gone by now. I hate to see you get hung for a crime you didn't remember committing. I'll tell you what I'm going to do. I'll marry you but with a couple of conditions. First, you have that old dog of yours fumigated and bathed. You help me run a legitimate business; that means no more hitting up the tourists for money and stay loyal to my interests. Plus, you will have to confess your crimes to the local Ladies Club and the Church so you can be forgiven and promise to never touch a lady like that again. If you break any of these promises I will swear the marriage was a scam and have you hauled off to jail." All the time she was saying this she was cracking up inside. *Finally! Someone got the better of the old con!*

Life can be weird though. Two years after they married, she died of a heart attack and left Jasper with more money than he knew what to do with. He left Parker for California and nobody saw him until, in his late 90's, he arrived in town broke, hungry, dirty and cold with a new set of scams to try out on the tourists. Some people never learn.

Chapter Twenty-six

Annoyingly Happy

Max, who just celebrated his 83rd birthday is in a good mood today. He's been in a good mood for as long as anyone can remember. He's one of those rare people that are endlessly sunshiny, annoyingly happy and if you are around him very long it will rub off on you too. You either love him or he drives you nuts depending on how much caffeine you consumed (or didn't consume) before running into him.

Max has owned the Parker Town Hardware Store for over sixty years. He was born here and so was his father who started the business when he was in his twenties.

My Wings Got Lost with the Luggage

Max loves serving the public and has made a very good living since his is the only hardware store for over 50 miles in any direction except for the little store in Crawford that is owned by Max's twin brother Sam. Sam is exactly like Max and when they get together it's a laugh fest.

Money is secondary to Max; in fact in over 50 years he has rarely seen the books. His wife of 55 years, Edna, won't let him near the accounts. She is absolutely honest but doesn't trust him with the files. Max is okay with the situation and feels secure knowing his wife is absolutely honest but still kids her about keeping a nest-egg in a bank in the Bahamas. She actually has a small account with plans to go to the islands for a vacation with her sons after Max passes. Max never had the desire to go anywhere and never missed the money.

Edna took over the business when they first got married. It took almost a year and a half to straighten out the mess Max had created and she wasn't about to let that happen again. She worked hard in the store office and at the same time raised three boys, four if you count Max. Two of her sons went off to California to *find the world* and the youngest took over the business when Max got too old to handle it.

Max has never officially retired and his son still writes him out a "paycheck" that he cashes every two weeks so he'll have "spending money." He hangs around the store and chats with everyone who comes in the door. He knows almost the whole town by first name and always gives the kids a lollipop or some little toy he bought at a wholesale show.

You would think everything was just wonderful in Max's world and according to Max, it is, but the problem is not the world, it's Max. This problem is not new. It's been going on for years in varying degrees. Max loves to take things apart but his skills for putting them back together are bordering on no skill at all. This would be fine if he kept his taking things apart to himself but he is always volunteering to help anybody who needs a hand.

His son inherited Max's gift for making people feel good and evaded trouble on more than one occasion with a smile and a good pat on the back. "Oh, you know my Dad!" he would say with a wink.

The rear of the hardware store has a fixit shop that was started by Rabbi David Feldman more years ago than anyone can remember. When he died suddenly, the shop stayed empty for a number of years and gathered dust. In the last few years it has been a junk overflow for just about everything.

Max got a wild hair one day from a picture he saw in the diner of the fixit shop. So he hired a couple of high school kids to clean it out. They discovered a very nice set of precision tools for fixing watches and a box full of larger tools good for just about anything else.

Max was in heaven. He started letting the public know that the "fixit shop" was back in business and he was the "chief fixit guy." People brought in all kinds of stuff; blenders, radios, washing machines, you name it. It was amazing to Max how many things needed his skills. He started unscrewing this and unbolting that. Pieces were scattered all over the workbenches and piled to the ceiling. He had no system to keep track of what was what or whose was whose. His bright smiling face and gentle positive attitude kept people bringing him things to repair but nobody ever got them back. Weeks went by and stuff piled up and soon complaints were reaching the front of the store. Nobody ever complained directly to Max. His son, who normally manages the store had gone on vacation and left his assistant, Marvin, in charge, figuring there would be no problems. The store had practically run itself for the last ten years or more; what could possibly happen?

Marvin didn't know what to do so he called Max's wife. Edna came down and found that she had the skill to put everything back in place. She and Max became a team. He takes it apart and she puts it back together. I guess sometimes you just have to put the right person into the right job. She was also, casually, without letting Max know, telling everyone to take their stuff to a local handyman named Tom Brooks who would fix it right at a cheap rate and do a great job. Slowly the business just petered out and Max, feeling satisfied that he had fixed everything in town that needed to be fixed, closed the door and went back to selling hardware.

Chapter Twenty-seven

Free Will and No Bills

You are probably wondering where I was between my untimely death in Parker Town and the present; a period of over a hundred years or so, earth-time.

Yes. This had crossed your mind? Good. I'm glad to hear you are still interested.

I was a ghost in Parker Town for a few weeks but since I was no longer a living part of the town I felt sad. There is a grieving period on this side too until you realize the larger picture. Some people hang on to grief longer than others but we all get over it sooner or later.

The light tunnel is a great mood elevator or more of an escalator so to speak. I found the tunnel and went towards the light and landed on the *Other Side.* Sorry details are, for reasons that I cannot discuss, classified. But I can tell you the *Other Side* still has all the quirky things that make us human and personalities are pretty much the same. Variety is the spice of life and the amount of variety here is staggering. God loves to create and has been doing it for eons. You just can't believe that you are now given the keys to such vast knowledge.

Wait until you see the Internet over here! If you made the right choices in your human life God extends the leash and gives you more to deal with and it's not all easy. Evil still exists just as always but is meant to give us choices. The bad things just make the good look better and vice-versa.

I decided to use my newfound freedom to travel. God gives you free will on this side too and only suggests things. He suggested I go listen to the great music of the universe and work on my musicianship. I always wondered if this was kind of a sideways complement but He was right. I listened to such a variety that sometimes I thought I would burst with appreciation; except for the time that stupid song, "Work Your Fingers to the Bone, What Do You Get? Bony Fingers," kept going through my head. I just about went nuts trying to get it to go away. The worst part was, I only knew half the words and had to hum the rest.

I visited planets that were just starting their musical careers by banging on rocks and found others that were performing by using thought and light patterns attached to extremely advanced high tech equipment. The intensity and feeling with which this music is played is almost overwhelming. It was a genuine mind-blower especially after just coming from 19th century Earth where minor chords are still giving musicians and theologians fits.

The same universe that makes you forget where you came from gives you back your memory when you die. All is connected. The dimension I live in is constantly expanding and new things are being added all the time. Eternity is a very large place. God said He can't help it. He keeps thinking up new stuff and loves to share it with others. I can't give away too many secrets here because it's the law but believe me, you are going to like what you see when you get here.

The lessons you learned on Earth are very important and will determine how you react to living on this side. So don't get in a hurry to come here. You may not have learned what you need to know to utilize *this* world to its capacity and could end up going back to Earth for more lessons.

One secret, if you want to call it that, or should I say well-known secret, is how much you need to learn to love. It will determine how many times you have to come back to the "Earth School" to get it right. Some people never learn and spend hundreds of lifetimes being miserable and making others miserable too. Others get it so fast they die in their sleep as a baby.

Chapter Twenty-eight
We All Live in Small Towns
No Matter How Big They Are

Writing this journal has given me a new appreciation for life in a little town like Parker because no matter where you are a human being can only focus on so much. Even in a city the size of New York a person who lives there still creates a nest in a tiny portion and calls it home. Maybe that's why they call sections of the city burrows. I'm not sure but it sounds good.

So everywhere I go, I find a microcosm of life that has the capability to shut out the big picture and enjoy the little things as if they were big. You know what they are;

a good umbrella on a rainy day, a smile from across the room during a difficult test, a tear in a friend's eye when she recalls a good time she spent with you. These are the things that matter and that's why I like about being an angel. Angels look at the little picture and know its value.

I am presently seeing Parker Town with what seems to be a whole new angelic vision. Walking down the street in invisible mode I not only see the buildings, I see the personalities that built them and the others that followed, the changes they made and things they left sacred.

Everyday seems the same in Parker Town but if you pay attention suddenly you see the leaves have dropped off the trees, Mrs. Kramer's hair is a little grayer. The kids you yelled at for breaking your picture window with a baseball are now coaching the little league with kids of their own. Time just keeps on moving and new surprises keep turning up. Every person you run into has a story or two. Or at least, has a borrowed one from some crazy old uncle.

These are the components that made writing this journal a wonderful experience. It has given me new perspective and appreciation for the little things ordinary people go through just to make it in this world. I now know why God had me write it. It wasn't for Him; it was for me, and you, whoever you are. Maybe you will see the grocer or the plumber or even the banker in a new light. Maybe you'll even try to find the story behind the title or uniform that he or she hides behind. Almost every person born is willing to share their story. All you have to do is ask.

Mark Griffin

A Little Note from God's Wife

Dear Griffin Marcus,

Glad you enjoyed writing the journal. We told you if you finished in time we had something in mind that you would really like. Here it is. You will be given, if you choose, the training, tools and talents to become an artist, a writer and illustrator for children. Your music is going to give you a firm foundation for the work ahead. As always, it's your choice but may I suggest that you open your mind to this idea. The rewards are endless and we'll cover the expenses. Let us know ASAP.

Love for Eternity, Mrs. G.

PS. There is a girl named Petunia who just passed over. We told her all about you and she wants to meet you. What do you think? Check with Molly.

A Few Sentimental
Thoughts from an Angel

Afterword:

I think I finally figured out why God wanted me to write this book. It wasn't to teach me discipline or give Him something to read; it was to show me that every human being no matter how big or small has a story of equal importance in the whole scheme of things. Life is a game of inches and every minute has value.

There are simple stories that, on the surface, look less important than others. Other stories are filled with such awesome details that they border on fantasy.

Some stories may not even have an obvious purpose in the present but have huge impacts on the future once you put all the pieces together.

I have always loved a good story but to be a fly on the wall when it happens is a rare privilege. It gave me a new view on the old saying: *You had to be there.*

I remember when I was a child lying in bed thinking about how wonderful it was to have a new pair of shoes just sitting on my bedroom floor waiting to be shown to my friends. Excitement comes in all sizes and shapes.

I spent some time selling RV's and could see that childlike wonder on the faces of the old couples who had saved their money for years to join the lifestyle of a gypsy. Some found it a lot different than they had anticipated and soon found the machine taking up space in a side yard waist-high in weeds. Others couldn't wait to find the magic, freedom, and wonders of the road.

I think this job of writing snippets from other peoples' lives is my way of traveling the world. It has given a new lease on my life and fresh excitement toward people of all walks of life, the more diverse the better.

My Wings Got Lost with the Luggage

I have played music most of my life and had the pleasure of traveling to some amazing places to present my version of live entertainment. Every time I get wrapped up in self-importance I think back to a night in at the MT in Parker Town when a young tourist with a cheap guitar showed up at the door. I proceeded to try to make him believe that I was one of the greatest guitarists he had ever heard and after several songs he even threw a few compliments my way that re-enforced my picture of myself. He then asked me if he could play something he had written. I brought my nose down out of the air and handed him the guitar with that *go ahead and try to impress the old pro look.* He proceeded to play a whole song using only one chord and darned if it didn't sound great and damned if I didn't know that chord. It just goes to show, you never know where that little tidbit is going to come from and how it's going to grow. I humbled down and got him to teach me that chord and I have used it ever since. Some of my best songs have been written around it and to this day I have no idea where that guy went or whatever happened to him.

If you are out there somewhere and read this I just want to say "thank you" for knocking me off my self-centered pedestal and for giving me a new appreciation for the little things.

Thank you, Mr. and Mrs. God for giving me this little project and the insight to see it through. I have gained a huge appreciation for individuals who just kept on going despite the odds. I enjoyed watching this project grow into a wonderful mish-mash of funny, heart-warming tales. Thank you for this experience we call *life* and the occupants who have made me laugh.

I don't know who to quote, so please forgive me:

"They say: *God must have a sense of humor. Look at the guy sitting next to you. And if you think you are just a bit too wonderful... Try looking in the mirror because you really are amazing.*"

-Griffin Marcus

About the Author:

Mark Griffin, 60, and his wife Patty, live in Desert Hot Springs, California. He is the author/illustrator of thirteen full-color children's books. A professional musician and songwriter; he sings and plays eleven instruments. He wrote all the songs and played all the instruments on three CDs. Also, recorded two CDs of country songs that date back to 1893. Two blues albums: Leonard Samartino and the Blues Mystics

Available at:

www.kidsbooksfree.com

www.amazon.com

E-mail: mark10550@verizon.net

Please look for his second novel on Amazon:

You Never See a Dead Cat Up a Tree

Thanks to Angels like Me

Mark Griffin

Made in the USA
Charleston, SC
15 November 2012